CHRISTMAS TREES AND MISTLETOE

JEANINE LAUREN

Littleford House Books

CHAPTER 1

It was still dark outside when Kathleen Johnson poured herself a cup of coffee and padded across the hardwood floor of her living room in her bunny slippers, a gift from her granddaughters the previous year. She stopped in front of the window, sipped the hot liquid, and looked down at the harbor.

The local sailing and boat club was nearly ready for the holiday festival of lights: the dozen or more boats moored in the harbor had multicolored lights strung from their decks to their masts, and the reflections sparkled delightfully on the water. They were ready for the Lights on the Harbor Sailpast, a decades-old tradition where the boats paraded past in their holiday splendor. It was scheduled to take place the first week of December, only nine days away.

Kathleen nodded her approval. This eagerly anticipated and well-attended event marked the beginning of the holiday season and brought much-needed foot traffic to the harbor—visitors who purchased gifts from the local merchants and her own well-stocked toy store.

She resisted the urge to think about work, enjoying instead the sun rising

There would be time enough for that when she got to the store. Meanwhile, she tried to calm her mind and enjoy the walk. It was a clear day, unusual this time of year. Sunshine Bay was, despite its name, rarely sunny between November and March, when a perpetual cloud covered the little town. The upside was that snow gathered on the mountaintops, to the delight of skiers and those, like herself, who liked to appreciate its beauty from afar. She walked through the streets, deserted except for vendors out making deliveries and other shopkeepers arriving to open their own stores. It reminded her of what she liked most—aside from being closer to her daughter and granddaughter— about living here on island: the slower pace of life.

Despite her attempts to focus on the moment, her thoughts drifted, as they often did, back to the store. She had worked hard this past year and was determined not to repeat last year's disastrous fourth quarter. This month, if she executed her marketing plan well, she would finally see the much-needed return on her investment in the business. And no one would ever have to know that she had been duped—again.

Her store, formerly Curious Kid Toys and Games, was the same store she had visited with her mother fifty years before. She had spent her allowance there on books and games, always careful to ask for educational toys she knew her mother would subsidize. Her mother, she thought now, would have approved of her purchasing the store, she had purchased, she realized that though the ten-year-average sales were indeed good, the operation had been losing money for the past two years. The store didn't have a website, a healthy customer base, or product people wanted to buy.

Drawing on her considerable volunteer experience raising money for hospitals, Kathleen realized she had to create a new brand and find new and repeat customers, or else the business would fail—and so, as Terrence had predicted, would she.

The bell over the door tinkled as she pushed it open and stepped over the threshold. The little bell was one of the few items she'd kept from the original decor, and she loved her store now. It was bright, colorful, and filled with educational toys and crafts. It smelled of new books with glossy covers. It was a place where children, teachers, and parents could find quality, user-friendly, and hard-to-source products. And they could get live demonstrations of some of the newer technology before purchasing.

Her market research, her time spent in the schools earlier in the year, the new name and website, and her semi-weekly sales bulletins with educational tips had all paid off. This month, if all went as expected, she could finally pay herself a living wage, hire another full-time clerk, and put the business firmly in the black.

But today, she reminded herself, was decoration day. It was a good use of a Thursday morning, as business was often slow in the early part of the day. Behind the counter was a box of

A month? Surely she had misheard. "How long will you be away?"

"They think two to three weeks. We're hoping to be home by Christmas."

"That's nearly five weeks away, honey." For a physician, her daughter had an appalling lack of time sense.

"Right, yes, I know. Umm..."

Kathleen shook her head. Her daughter sounded scattered. Nicole had too much to deal with this morning, and she didn't need her mother adding to her problems.

"Listen, dear." She glanced up at the clock. "I just need to wait a few minutes until Jackie gets here." She was going to need more help to pull this off. Maybe her two part-timers, Casey and Josh, could start taking on more hours. She made a mental note to follow up with them that afternoon.

The tiny bell over the door tinkled. Her assistant manager and right-hand person, Jackie, stepped into the store, two coffees in hand, grinning and ready to take on the day.

"Oh, great," said Kathleen, reaching for the coffee. "Listen, honey, Jackie just stepped in. I'll be there soon." She took a coffee cup from Jackie's outstretched hand and mouthed the words *thank you*.

She clicked off the phone and gave Jackie a quick update before hurrying home to get her car. Her daughter needed her. It was the first time that had happened since the twins had been born ten years earlier. It would be hard to juggle the kids and the store, but she would make it work.

For Nicole.

CHAPTER 2

Roy Davies was jogging through Sunshine Bay Park with his friend Patrick, enjoying the swish of the dead leaves that swirled out of his way as he passed.

This was the sixth week in a row he had been running again, and every week it got easier. Today he was going fast enough to feel a trickle of sweat run down his back under his fleece jacket, but slow enough that he could still speak. Well, sputter. Which is what he did when Patrick brought up his favorite topic.

"Why don't you come out with me this weekend? You can be my wingman," said Pat.

"Wingman! Are you nuts? I don't want to hang around with you while you cruise for your next conquest."

"Come on, it's not like that. I just need someone to come and have a drink with me at the pub, maybe chat up a couple of women if we happen to meet them. No strings. No pressure."

"I don't know. I'm not ready."

"It's been two years," Pat said. "Lois wouldn't have wanted you to be alone, you know."

"How do you know what Lois would have wanted?"

Pat slowed to a walk and turned toward him. "If you must know, I spoke to Lois. She made me promise to encourage you when I thought the time was right."

"You spoke to Lois? My wife is in her grave, Pat. Surely she's not still managing me."

"I visited her in the hospice one day," Pat said, vaguely. "She asked me to come."

Roy dropped to a walk, grateful for the reprieve to catch his breath.

"She did? Let me guess—she asked you to check up on me, make sure I take my vitamins, and watch my weight."

"Of course. Now, about that weight," said Pat, tapping him on the arm. "You ready to pick up the pace now?"

"Sure," Roy said, thinking that he could really use another ten-minute break. Though he now had a regular jogging routine, he was still nowhere near Pat's level of fitness. Pat was a regular gym rat who could probably still fit into the jeans he'd worn in his twenties. He also still had a full head of hair, unlike Roy, who had to wear a toque to cover his naked head and stay warm. "But I'm not sure I'm ready to be anyone's wingman."

"Think about it. I thought we could go to the singles dance. You know, the one they hold down at the community hall every month."

"A single's dance? That's a far cry from a drink at the local pub." He couldn't go to a singles dance. He was married… No, he corrected himself: he was widowed. Technically single, but he couldn't see himself with another woman, even if it was only on the dance floor. He wasn't ready. He doubted he would ever be ready to let another woman into his life.

"It's only a dance. You used to be pretty good when you were younger," Pat said, picking up the pace again.

"That was over forty years ago. I can't dance to today's music."

"Don't worry, the music's still the same. They play stuff from the seventies and eighties."

Roy laughed. Pat had an answer for everything. "I'll think about it." His cell phone rang, and he slowed to pull it out of his pocket.

"It's Jason. I'll catch up with you," he said. He slowed to a walk to answer his son's call, secretly glad for another excuse to take a break. He was tired this morning. Heck, he was tired every morning lately.

"Dad, It's Jason. Remember when I asked if you would watch the kids when we had to go on an emergency trip, and you said yes?"

"It was only a month ago. I don't have dementia, Jason."

"Yes, well, there's been an earthquake in Italy, and they've asked Nicole and I to go. We're leaving this afternoon—joining the rest of the team in Vancouver and getting oriented before we leave on the red-eye."

"I'll be there as soon as I can. Just in the park, here, practicing my jogging."

"Great! Thanks, Dad."

Roy put his phone back in his pocket and jogged after Patrick to tell him the news.

"Let me know if you need any help," Patrick said.

"Thanks. I'm sure we'll be okay for a week. Can we make our run a little later tomorrow? Nine, maybe? After the girls are at school."

He jogged back to his truck and paused a few minutes behind the wheel to catch his breath. He really needed to see a doctor. If Lois were still there, she would have nagged him into it by now.

But Lois, his life partner of over forty years, was gone, leaving him alone to build a life without her. He turned the key in the ignition.

At least he had Jason and his wife and the grandkids. The little family was his responsibility now. Lois had been adamant about that, one of the last times he had seen her in hospice. "They'll need you when I'm gone. You make sure you're always there for them." Had she known that he would need them as much as they needed him? Probably. Lois had always known things before he did.

Besides, if he was looking after the kids, he couldn't be Patrick's wingman, and he wouldn't have to try dancing again.

When Roy pulled into his son's driveway after grabbing an overnight bag and a shower, he was chagrined, though not surprised, to find Nicole's mother's red Mini in the driveway. Of course Nicole had called Kathleen. And Kathleen would be in her element now, pushing her way into this situation.

Didn't they think he could handle this himself? It was only a couple of ten-year-olds, after all. And only a week. Besides, that woman had a business to run.

He climbed out of his truck and bent over with an *oof* as a flying figure with brown pigtails ran into him, squeezing him around his middle.

"Grandpa! You're here!"

"Hi, Jade," he said, patting her on the top of her head. "I guess it's just me and you two for the next while, eh?"

"And Nana," said Jade excitedly.

"Right. Nana," he added. Aware Jade was watching, he reined in his frustration and quickened his step. He'd better get in there and find out what they'd been planning in his absence. He didn't want to dance to Kathleen's tune for the next week.

"Can we work out in the shop when you're here?" Jade asked, skipping along beside him. "I want to refinish that chair we got from the garage sale last time. Mom said it looks just like the one she had when she was little."

"Okay," he said. "We can do that." Good. A project. That would keep Jade busy and possibly Amber as well, though Amber, Jade's fraternal twin, was more interested in design and color than in the hard work of sanding and polishing. Amber had been closer to Lois than to him, and with Lois gone, he had to work harder to find something they could do together.

Jason stepped out onto the porch, greeting him with a hug and taking his bag.

"Hi, Dad. Thanks for doing this."

"I see Kathleen's here as well," said Roy.

"Nicole thought it best if you were a tag team. Trust me, with those two, you'll be glad for the help."

"I don't want her kind of help. She'll have me twisted into a pretzel with her damn 'organizing'..."

Jason turned to Jade. "Go in and get ready for school. We'll be leaving soon." They watched her scamper up the steps, and then Jason turned back to Roy.

"Dad, what is it with you and Kathleen? So what if she's organized? What's wrong with that?"

"Why don't you just tell her we don't need her help after all? It's only a week. I looked after you for a week alone before."

"Actually, Dad, it's closer to a month than a week. We'll be lucky if we get home by Christmas."

"A month?"

"Yes, that's why we've asked Kathleen to help."

"Wasn't there anyone else you could ask?"

"Not on an hour's notice, no." Jason paused with his hand on the front-door handle. "Listen. I need you to put this feud, or whatever it is that's going on between you two, away while we're gone. It's not good for the kids to see the tension. Can't you just get along?"

"Of course," he said, then muttered to himself, "as long as she stays out of my way."

"I heard that," Jason said. "I need you to promise, Dad."

Roy pulled his hand over his face, trying to organize his thoughts. "I promise... as long as she does her part."

"I'm holding you to it," said Jason. "Nicole and I will have enough to worry about." Then he opened the door and led the way inside.

Roy followed, stopping on the threshold when he saw the object of his consternation. Kathleen Brown. No.

Kathleen Johnson now. The same woman who had broken his wife's heart. They'd been best friends, Kathleen and Lois. And then, for no apparent reason, right after his and Lois's wedding, Kathleen had cut ties, not once looking back.

"Hello, Roy," Kathleen said, her voice brittle. *Good.* At least she wasn't happy about this either.

"Kathleen." He nodded coolly in her direction, trying to ignore her piercing brown eyes. He knew those eyes from their childhood. Inquisitive, knowing eyes. And right now, she seemed to think she knew all about him.

She walked over and smiled, sticking out her hand. What did she think this was? One of her networking events? Jason was watching, so he reluctantly shook her hand and managed not to bare his teeth. She always got under his skin. She had been able to do that even when they were children growing up down the street from each other.

"I guess we'll be working together on this," she said, as though this were any other business arrangement.

"I thought I was staying here alone," he growled, earning a frown from Jason. The last thing he needed was to share a roof with the woman.

"I'm checking in after work and helping. But I'd be happy to stay here instead if you like."

"You'll be checking up on me? I am not a child."

"No, I'll be helping you out, you big oaf. When was the last time you looked after two children for a month?" She stepped closer to him, her finger raised.

"So now you think I can't do it alone?" She was too close, so he poked his finger in her direction, trying to get her to back off while making his point.

"Well, since you asked—"

"No." Jason stepped between them and pushed them apart with his arms. "This will stop now!"

Roy looked up at his son, suddenly embarrassed, and then at Kathleen, her face flushed bright red. What was it about her that always made him behave so badly?

Nicole interrupted his thoughts when she flew into the room to give him a hug. "I can't thank you enough for doing this, Dad. I know it's a lot to ask of both of you. Mom's agreed to check in after store hours and give you a break. And maybe do some of the cooking and ferrying the children around? Come to the kitchen. I've put the list of activities on the fridge, and"—she handed a couple of sheets of paper to each of them—"I've printed copies so you can coordinate."

Roy looked at the paper in his hand and followed his daughter-in-law into the kitchen. A spreadsheet. He hated spreadsheets. It was the thing he missed least about working as a hospital administrator. Spreadsheets reminded him of rules, constraints, and working to other people's expectations. All the things he appreciated leaving behind when he retired.

He watched Kathleen from a safe distance across the room. Her eyes were positively gleaming with excitement as she scanned the spreadsheets. Of course she'd love them. She even had a pen out now to make notes in the margin. No wonder Nicole was always planning. She'd caught this crazy affliction from her managing mother!

As he listened to Nicole go over the details, he noticed Kathleen smiling like a Cheshire cat full of secrets. He could tell that once the kids left, she would be ready to pounce on any opportunity to wheedle her way into more time with the kids. She'd try to make them forget about their other grandmother.

Lois would not be forgotten.

Not on his watch.

CHAPTER 3

Kathleen listened to Nicole with as much concentration as she could muster with that man standing across the room. Did he have to look so smug? He was still winning the favorite grandparent prize by being asked to stay under the same roof with the girls. It wasn't surprising. Jason and Nicole had always relied on his parents more when the children were born. The children knew Roy better. But she would make up for lost time. She had a month to plan activities with the girls. They were going to have fun.

She just wished the girls would hang off her the way Jade was hanging off Roy now. Jade loved her grandfather. They did projects together out in the shed, Jade had told her. And he was always showing her how to build or fix something.

Amber had been Lois's girl. Lois, who was a domestic goddess, could make a house a home just by walking into it. Kathleen had always envied that gift. For years, she failed at baking—her pie crust was never as flaky as Lois could make it —failed at keeping the house tidy—she was always too involved in projects and her husband's practice to do it thoroughly—and gardening? Nothing grew until Kathleen learned to contract out the best help. Managing others was her gift. Unfortunately, it wasn't a gift her granddaughters, nor her daughter, could appreciate.

No. They had loved Lois, who had always taken charge without seeming to. She wore a cloak of calm and ease, while Kathleen was tense and driven. Lois had a way of making everything look easy and bringing everything together. Her house looked like the pages of a magazine, and everyone gravitated toward her. She was a welcoming mother hen who took everyone under her wing.

Kathleen, on the other hand, used spreadsheets to plan, stayed on top of all the details, and was never rewarded. One former acquaintance had told her she wasn't surprised Chris had left her for another. "You need to learn to relax," the woman said. "You're always such a prickly pear. Everyone says so." Not soft and cuddly like Lois had been. Prickly. But not so prickly that comments like that hadn't hurt. They were one of the reasons she had moved back to Sunshine Bay—to get away from Chris's crowd and find a way to remove her outer shell. This month she would work even harder. These girls would adore her when she was done.

"Mom, did you have questions about the schedule?" Nicole was talking to her, and she focused on the paper in front of her for a moment, pretending to peruse it.

"It all looks pretty self-explanatory," she said after a moment. Spreadsheets were something she had taught her daughter to use, and she knew from experience that Nicole was thorough. If she had questions later, the answers would be in these pages, or she could ask the girls. She wouldn't need to consult with Roy at all.

"Jade," Nicole said, tapping the girl's shoulder to get her attention. "Go see if your father needs any more help, okay?"

"All right." Jade hugged her grandfather tight and then pulled herself away and ran upstairs.

"Now, there's one more thing," Nicole said, narrowing her eyes and glaring at Kathleen before turning to frown at Roy, who mirrored her expression. "You two have to promise me you will get along. I've told the girls they need to behave for you, so please"—she looked from one of them to the other—"behave yourselves. I don't want to have to worry about the tension here while I'm gone."

"Don't worry about us," Kathleen said. "We're both adults. We promise to play nice. Right, Roy?"

"You'll get no problems from me," Roy mumbled in his deep voice.

"Thanks, Mom, Roy." Nicole pulled them each into a hug. "This means so much to me."

"Well now, that's settled," Kathleen said. "I think it's time we made sure you have everything you need. Your plane leaves in a few hours, and you need to get to the airport."

"Girls!" Nicole said. "Grab your gear. It's time for school. Grandpa's going to drive you, so you aren't late." She turned to Roy and handed him a note. "Make sure the school gets this. They'll be a bit late this morning."

"What about Nana?" Amber asked.

"Nana's going to drop your dad and I at the airport and then go back to run the store. She'll be back to check in on you three tonight. Now give us a hug." She pulled the two girls into an embrace. "You be good while we're gone. We'll call you as often as we can, but don't worry if you haven't heard from us for a while."

"We know about the time difference, Mom," said Amber, her voice wavering a little.

"And that the Internet may be spotty," said Jade.

"You be good for Nana and Grandpa," said Nicole.

"We will," they chimed together.

"Come on, Amber," said Jade. Amber ran back to her mother and hugged her one last time before tearing after her sister to say goodbye to their father. They were soon climbing into their grandfather's truck and driving to school.

"Mom, thanks for agreeing to get along with Roy. I don't know what it is between you two, but I appreciate you putting it aside while we're gone."

"Anything for you, you know that." Kathleen pulled her daughter into a hug and stepped back to look at her. "Now, have you got all your things? Made all your arrangements? We should get you to the airport so you don't miss the plane to Vancouver. The last thing you'll want to do today is take a ferry."

"I'm on it," said Nicole, and she ran from the room to help Jason finish packing.

Roy came back a few minutes after dropping the kids off at school, and he helped Jason take their suitcases outside.

"I can take them to the airport if you like, Kathleen," he said. "I know you probably have work to do."

"Oh, you'd like me to leave, wouldn't you?" She wanted to be the one to take them to the airport, to show that she would be there for them.

"No," he grumbled, "I was thinking that this is your busy season at the store, and that the drive is going to take a while. That's all." He stood there, all six feet of him, making sense and looking good. Better than he had looked in high school with a full head of perpetually messy hair.

He cocked an eyebrow at her like he had when they were younger, when he used to tease her. She flushed, remembering those days. She would deliberately find reasons to spend time in the backyard while he and his brother lifted weights across the fence. She had crushed on him for years only to be treated like what she was: his friend, the girl next door. Not the girl he wanted.

Oh, to heck with him. He was right. She did need to be at the store. "You have a point," she said abruptly. "I'll say my goodbyes now and get back to the store. I'll be here this evening to see how you're doing and to tuck them in. Don't forget, they need to finish all their homework."

"I'm sure we'll manage," he said with a scowl.

She scowled back at him and walked out of the room to find her daughter. The less time she spent alone with Roy Davies, the better. The man irritated the heck out of her.

Climbing into her red Mini, Kathleen drove back to the store to relieve Jackie and figure out who else could help in the coming weeks. Hopefully business would be up so she could afford the extra help.

She smiled upon entering the shop, grateful to find it busy for a Thursday morning. Next week would be the last week of November, and the holiday season was now upon them. It was also American Thanksgiving, and several tourists visited Sunshine Bay on their way to watch the winter storms on the west coast or ski at Mount Washington.

"Your latest newsletter really worked. Everyone wants that new robot toy you brought in," said Jackie, after helping the last customer at the till. "I haven't had time to finish the ordering or the receiving, much less start decorating."

"I thought people would like that one, especially when Josh put it up on YouTube so people could see how easy it is to program. A five-year-old could do it."

"Is Josh almost finished school? We could really use his help. And Casey too."

"I was thinking about that on my way back. My daughter will be out of town for a few weeks and has asked me to help watch my granddaughters." She saw Jackie's frown and quickly added, "I'll work on the schedule tonight. Casey and

Josh have proven to be reliable workers. I'll speak to them both to see if they can start the Christmas season a bit earlier this year."

"That's a good idea. We haven't been this busy for years. You've really turned this place around since you took over."

"No. We've turned it around," Kathleen said. "I couldn't have done it without you."

"If you get Josh and Casey to come in this weekend, maybe they could help with the decorating. It's been hard to get that done with so much traffic."

"That's a great idea. They're a creative pair. Now, why don't you take a break and then go out to the back and take care of the stock? If it gets busy again up here, I'll call you."

"Do you want a coffee from the bakery? I'm going over to grab my breakfast."

"Yes, please." A third cup of coffee would be just the thing to pick up her waning energy this morning. "Here, it's my turn to buy." She pulled money for the coffee from her pocket and handed it to Jackie, then turned to help the next customer.

Jackie returned half an hour later, just as another batch of customers was leaving, and placed the coffee on the counter. "It's busy at the bakery, too. People are making it a regular shopping day."

"Hopefully this is the start to a good sales month," Kathleen said. "Now, you go out the back and unpack the boxes. We're getting low on stock on some of those shelves."

The rest of the day went by as briskly as it had started, which helped Kathleen keep her mind off her daughter traveling to an earthquake zone—and off the man staying with her grandchildren.

After closing and locking the door behind her last customer, Kathleen hummed along to "Jingle Bells" on the radio while cashing out the till and reconciling the receipts. Her cell phone rang, and, seeing Nicole's name on the call display, she answered it immediately.

"Mom, I've just talked to the kids, and they say Roy is resting. Could you check in on them?" Nicole sounded concerned.

"I'll be on my way as soon as I finish closing up shop and going to the bank." She smiled to herself. So the girls had been too much for Roy to handle after all. She took up a stack of twenties and re-counted them while she listened to Nicole.

"Could you also make sure the kids don't watch the news for the next few days?" Nicole asked. "There have been some aftershocks, and the footage is pretty graphic. I don't want them to worry."

"I'll do that. What time does your plane leave?"

"In a couple of hours."

"I'm sure you will do great work there."

"I know. I just wish…"

"I'll check in on them every day, and I have help coming in at the store so I can be there for them. Don't worry about the kids."

"It's not that. It's... I wasn't going to tell you this, but after talking to the kids, I think I should."

Kathleen stopped counting the money. "What's wrong?"

"I'm not sure anything is really wrong, but Roy... I wish Jason had said something earlier."

"What's wrong?"

"Jason is worried about Roy's health. That's why he was so quick to agree that you should help with the kids this month. Roy's been tired a lot lately. Jason thinks there may be something wrong."

"I see." She didn't want this information. As much as Roy bothered her, he was a proud man and wouldn't want her to know about his problems. She hoped the kids hadn't told him about her own challenges in the past two years. She shuddered a little at the thought of how much of her private business had been shared with others. But divorce did that. It cracked open a marriage so everyone could pick the parts they wanted and discard the parts—and people—they didn't need anymore. *Enough, you old fool,* she admonished herself, frowning at her momentary lapse into wallowing and turning her attention back to the conversation.

"I know this is a lot to ask, but could you spend a bit of time with them on the weekends? I think two days straight with the kids may be too much for him."

"Of course. They can even spend next Saturday at my place. It's the sailpast."

"That's a great idea!" Nicole sounded relieved. "I knew I could count on you to watch him without making it seem obvious. Thanks, Mom."

"I'll call you back later tonight after I've been to see them, okay? Meanwhile, you should get some rest. I expect you'll need it when you get there."

"Yes, I'm going to take a nap before I have to catch our next plane. Love you, Mom."

"I love you too." She hung up and quickly re-counted the money, confirming the amounts before putting the float in the safe and the rest in a bag to go into the bank's night deposit. She would drop it off on the way to Nicole's house then check in on the kids.

And Roy.

It was hard to think of Roy, the boy who had lived next door to her since they were six, having any health problems. He had always been so strong, so easygoing. Her best friend—until Lois had moved just down the street. Then Lois became the one she shared everything with. Her hopes, her dreams, everything... even how she felt about Roy.

Roy was never jealous of her bond with Lois. Instead, he had welcomed Lois, and they had been a trio for much of high school. Others were welcomed into their little group, but in the end, it was the three of them who had been inseparable.

Adrenaline was coursing through her when she finally stepped onto Nicole's porch. She had thought through Nicole's words as she drove over, reframing what she had heard into a more benign possibility. Roy was probably just resting to get his second wind before tackling dinner and getting the girls through their homework. He was probably fine.

She would just pop in for a few minutes, check that everything was going well, then spend an hour at the shop on the way home, confirming the order for her new stock and putting the finishing touches on her newsletter. Then she would be off to bed early. Confident that all would be well, she raised her hand to knock on the door, only to have it open before her knuckles could connect with the wood.

Amber peeked out with a finger to her lips. "Shhh. We don't want to wake him," she said, beckoning Kathleen forward and past the living room, where Roy was lying on the couch, snoring loud enough to wake the neighbors. She paused a moment to look at him. It had been a long time since she had seen Roy asleep. The last time had been years ago, when she and Lois had gone camping a few weeks before graduation. Remembering that night was still painful. That night she discovered the truth that would break her heart and catapult her away from Sunshine Bay for the next four decades.

Amber tugged her hand, and, turning her attention back to the job at hand, Kathleen followed her granddaughter to the kitchen.

"What's going on?" she gasped, stepping over a splotch of tomato sauce into the once-clean kitchen. She surveyed the carnage. Tomato sauce streaked the floor from one end of the room to the other, with a large puddle near the sink. Vegetables—zucchini, mushrooms, green peppers, and onion skins—were everywhere. She looked from Amber to Jade, waiting for an answer. This never would have happened if Roy were awake. *Damn him!*

"We're making dinner," said Jade excitedly. "Spaghetti and garlic bread." She was standing in front of the family bread machine, filling it with flour.

"You girls shouldn't be using the stove on your own."

"We didn't. We were waiting for you," Amber said. "But we thought we would help get ready. Mom told us to be helpful."

Kathleen stepped over to the counter, where the girls had arranged little piles of chopped mushrooms, onions, celery, and green peppers on a cutting board. A gadget they had used to chop was sitting nearby. The meat was defrosting on a plate on the counter. She breathed a small sigh of relief. At least they hadn't been using knives.

"Why didn't you wake your grandfather?"

"He's tired. He took Jade out to play soccer after school and then showed me how to do some of my math problems," Amber said. "He said he needed to lie down for a few minutes and to wake him in half an hour, but—"

"He looked pretty tired," Jade cut in, "and we knew you were coming soon anyway. Grandpa isn't a great cook, you know. Grandma used to do all the cooking."

"Besides," Jade went on, "it's not like we don't know how to cut vegetables. We help Mom and Dad with dinner all the time."

"And we have the recipe book." Amber held up the book to show her, spreading a puff of flour into the air.

Kathleen held up both her hands and laughed, delighted by their enthusiasm. "Okay, okay. I see you've done a lot here, but we need to clear up this mess." She pointed at the tomato sauce, the flour, the onion skins.

"Yes, Nana." The girls' smiles fell, and she immediately felt guilty for dampening their enthusiasm. They needed to feel like they were helping, and they needed to be kept busy or they would begin to miss their parents. And worry.

"It's important for a cook to have a clean place to work. Let's clear the counter of all the peelings. When we've got the sauce simmering, you two can take turns mopping up the floor."

"We don't know how to mop up floors," protested Jade.

"Your Mom never showed you how to mop floors?" Kathleen laughed. "She probably wanted all that fun for herself." Her plan worked: the pair looked excited at the prospect of learning to mop. "As soon as we're finished cooking, I'll teach you."

She placed her coat and bag on the kitchen chair and walked to the sink to wash her hands. "Have you got any other bread that we could use to make garlic bread? This bread you have started will take a while."

Amber nodded vigorously and went to the cupboard where the bread was kept. "Here, Nana. We can use this."

"Wonderful. Now we'll need some butter, garlic powder, and tinfoil." She showed the girls how to butter the bread and turned on the oven before putting the foil-wrapped bread inside. Then they browned the meat, added in the ingredients, and tossed in the spices. Fifteen minutes later, after the spaghetti sauce was simmering on the stove and she had started the heat under the pot of water the girls had made ready for the pasta, Roy came down the hall.

"What's going on in here? I asked you to wake me." He staggered into the room, rubbing sleep from his eyes, just as Kathleen turned.

"Stop!" she yelled but it was too late. He stepped into the tomato sauce, and his leg went out from under him, bringing him down on his back.

"Are you okay?" She ran past both girls, who stood with wide eyes, and was at his side in a moment. He was lying there, stunned, his head in the hall and his feet in the kitchen.

"What happened?" he muttered, before his eyes fluttered shut.

Kathleen reached out and patted his shoulder. "Roy, can you hear me?" She heard a small whimper behind her. She needed to stay calm so as not to worry the girls. "Roy." She shook his shoulder. "Can you hear me, Roy?"

He opened his eyes and stared at her. "What are you doing here?" He struggled to sit up, and she reached around his shoulders to help him.

"Slowly, now. You've had a nasty fall." She hoped he didn't have a concussion.

He was sitting now, legs spread wide, hands behind him, holding himself upright and gazing steadily at her with his dark-brown eyes. Then he slowly looked around at the mess, at the girls. "What are you three up to?"

He was trying to be nonchalant, thought Kathleen, and she nearly giggled.

Jade slipped to the floor beside him. "Are you okay, Grandpa?" She was patting his arm, and he smiled wanly at her.

"I'll be fine."

Amber was crying now. "I'm so sorry. I opened the can, and it slipped."

"What's that smell?" Roy asked, wrinkling his nose.

"Oh, no!" Kathleen sprang to her feet and ran to the oven, nearly losing her footing on the same tomato sauce before opening the oven to a cloud of smoke. She grabbed a tea towel and pulled out the bread, dropping the crispy package on the stove beside the simmering sauce and boiling noodles.

The smoke billowed out from the oven, setting off the fire alarm. *Screeeeech!* She put her hand over her ears and looked around for something to fan the smoke away from the smoke detector. "I can help, Nana!" Jade was up on a chair with a cookie sheet held above her head near the detector. "I help Mom with this all the time!"

The noise finally subsided, and Kathleen turned to make sure the stove and burners were off to avoid further mishaps. Then she heard the deep rumble of laughter coming from the floor behind her, followed by giggles from two little girls. She turned to see them all there on the floor, the girls hanging off their grandfather, laughter having overtaken them, and she couldn't help but smile.

"This is all your fault, Roy," she said, only half-angry.

"I know. I'll help clear up. But first, let's eat."

"Can we eat in the dining room?" Amber asked. "There's not as much smoke in there."

"Come here, then," Kathleen laughed. "Everyone, line up. We'll load up our plates here at the stove and go in the other room."

The girls scampered to their feet and went to get cutlery and plates while Kathleen poured the spaghetti into a colander. She spooned the sauce over spaghetti noodles and handed the girls their plates before turning to take an empty plate from Roy.

"Kathleen, how long have you been here?"

"Not long. Got here just in time to put together the sauce." She handed him a knife and fork with the plate.

"Thank you for making dinner," he said.

"How's your head?" she asked. "You took a bit of a fall."

"I'm okay. Feeling rather silly, if you must know. I'm sorry I wasn't watching them closely enough."

"I'm sorry I didn't clean up that sauce right away. I was going to do it right after the food was on to simmer."

They stood gazing at each other a moment longer before Kathleen stepped backward to get a plate from the cupboard. "You go on ahead. I'll be there in a minute."

He went into the other room and came back almost immediately. "Do you want something to drink? The girls are both going to have orange juice." He walked to the fridge to pull out the bottle.

"I'll just have a glass of water," she said, reaching for a glass in the cupboard. He only had two hands. She could get her own water.

"Okay," he said, standing back, hands in the air in surrender. "You grab yours. I'll be right in."

She walked to the door and pushed it open with her back, glancing at him bent over the glasses, pouring out juice, tomato sauce all over his pant leg. Now that he was okay, she took a moment to smile to herself. It had been pretty funny.

They ate in silence for a moment, all the mirth in the other room settling into contentment.

"This is good, Nana," said Amber.

"It's just like the way Mom makes it," said Jade.

"I miss Mom," Amber said. "Do you think they're there yet?"

Her question reminded Kathleen of her earlier conversation with Nicole. "They're leaving Vancouver tonight, so they won't be there until tomorrow. Why don't we call them after we finish the clean-up?" Kathleen said.

Amber picked up the dishes as soon as they finished eating, and Jade rushed to help her, though it wasn't her turn. Kathleen showed them how to mop a floor, and soon the kitchen was spotless but for a few wayward spots of tomato sauce on the wall. Kathleen dialed her daughter's cell phone and was happy to hear her sounding much more rested, and much less tense, than the last time they spoke.

"I was just going to call you," Nicole said. "How are things?"

"We're fine. The girls just wanted to say hello," she said. "Here's Amber." She handed the phone to Amber, who was standing closest to her, and the twins scrambled onto the love seat in the living room to talk to their parents.

"Thank you again for dinner." Roy's deep voice rumbled from just behind her left ear, causing her to jump.

"It was no trouble. I would have had to cook dinner for myself anyway." She would take the high ground as she dealt with him this month. He was probably tired from amusing the girls all afternoon. Once he'd been at it for a day or so, he would get used to the new routine.

"Well, I appreciate it," he said, watching the girls as they told their parents about their day. "It's been a long time since I watched children. In fact, I don't know that I've ever watched them without Lois."

Of course he would bring Lois into the conversation. She was always in the conversation.

"Once the girls are settled and I get their lunch together for tomorrow, I should be going. I still have more work to do tonight," she said, stepping back and putting more distance between them. He smelled of grass and earth and sweat— and tomato sauce. Not an unpleasant smell, but it was making her feel things she hadn't felt in a while.

"Grandpa, Dad wants to talk to you." Amber ran to give the phone to Roy, interrupting their silent standoff. Flustered, Kathleen returned to the kitchen.

She had barely laid the bread out on the counter to make sandwiches when Roy appeared with the phone and handed it to her. "Nicole wants to speak to you."

"Thanks." She took the phone, and he left the kitchen again.

"Mom, is Roy still there?"

"No, did you want him?"

"No, I wanted to ask you how you found things when you got to the house. The girls told me he fell asleep before dinner." Nicole was sounding overwhelmed again. She needed reassurance, so Kathleen summoned her most soothing voice.

"I'm sure he just overdid it today. He's not used to watching two active girls. I promise I'll come by every day after work and make sure the girls are okay. And I'll remind them they have my cell number in case of emergency. If necessary, I can come and stay a few nights. We'll be fine."

"Okay. It's just that... we'll be so far away..."

"And you'll be doing important work. We're all proud of you, Nicole. Don't worry. I'm here." She heard the rumble of Jason's voice in the background.

"I have to go now," Nicole said. "Thanks for being there, Mom. We couldn't do this without you."

"Think nothing of it," Kathleen said. "We'll be fine. We'll all be just fine." She would make sure of it.

The phone clicked off, and she set it down on the kitchen counter before going back to making lunches.

"Nana, what are you doing?" She looked up to find Amber standing in the kitchen doorway.

"Making your lunch for tomorrow. Can you tell me where your lunch boxes are?"

Amber ran to the cupboard, pulled out the boxes, showed her where to find the waxed food wrappers, then helped Kathleen pack the boxes for the next day.

"Where's Jade?"

"She's playing a video game with Grandpa."

"You don't play?"

"Oh, I do, but I'd rather read a book. Mom bought me a whole series about horses last week. I can't wait to read them."

"If you run out of books, let me know. You can come and see if there are any at the store you might like."

Amber beamed. "Really? Maybe after I finish this series and the one my friend is reading about wizards. We swap them when we're done."

"Well, let me know if there are others you might like. Maybe Santa will bring you one."

Amber laughed. "Okay, Santa—I mean Nana. I'll let you know."

"And what does your sister like, do you think?"

"Probably a new tennis racket or something. I'll ask her tomorrow."

Kathleen put the lunch into the fridge and glanced up at the clock. It was already eight thirty. Her early night was going to be a late night after all.

"Time for you girls to get ready for bed," she said to Amber. "I have to go home now."

"Okay, Nana. See you." And the girl scampered off to talk to Jade and, presumably, to read another chapter of her book.

As she was leaving, Kathleen paused to speak to Roy. "How are you? You took quite a knock to the head."

"I have a pretty hard head," he said. "I'll be okay."

"You don't think you have a concussion?"

"I'm okay. I was just surprised is all. Don't worry."

"Could you call me in the morning, just to let me know you are okay?"

He looked at her, sweeping his gaze around her face. "Thanks for your concern, Kathleen. I'll be fine. Don't worry."

She nodded, knowing that if their situations were reversed, she would probably refuse to call him too. She was glad the girls had her phone number.

"I'm not sure if Nicole told you, but she asked me to make sure the girls didn't watch the news for a while. There've been aftershocks, and she doesn't want them to worry."

He nodded, face sober. "They will have quite the job ahead of them, those two. Don't worry, I'll keep the girls away from the news."

"Thank you," she said. "I appreciate it."

"Anything for Nicole and the girls," he said, turning his attention to the television and flipping on the news. "Don't forget to lock the door when you leave, okay?"

She turned and walked out without another word, seething all the way home. After covering for him with Nicole, all he could do was dismiss her. What a jerk!

CHAPTER 4

The next morning, Roy woke late, feeling
as though he'd just fallen asleep, and
dragged himself out of bed to face the day.
His body ached all over from the fall, and
he rubbed the good-sized goose egg on the
back of his head. He hadn't had one of
those in years. He showered before going
to wake the kids and examined the
growing bruise on his hip. Maybe he would
beg off his run with Patrick this morning.

On his way downstairs, he knocked on the girls' bedroom doors until he heard a strangled "coming" from Amber and a perky "yep!" from Jade, who bounced down the stairs only a few minutes behind him.

"Where's your sister?"

"She fell asleep again."

"Was she reading last night?" he asked, remembering that Nicole sometimes took away Amber's book at night if she wasn't sleeping.

"I dunno," answered Jade. Of course, she probably wouldn't tell him even if she knew.

"I see," he said, pulling granola from the cupboard and milk from the fridge. "Could you go up and make sure she's really coming? I don't want you two to be late for school."

He pulled their lunches from the fridge and placed them on the counter, begrudgingly thankful for Kathleen's help the night before. He needed to thank her for that when he saw her later. She had saved the day, and she had said nothing about him falling asleep on the job, which wasn't like her. Normally she would have thrown it in his face. Maybe his fall had saved him from a blistering dressing-down. He rubbed at his hip and smiled. The bruise was probably the lesser of the two evils.

Her competitive nature was something he had never understood. It wasn't like the girls would love her less if they loved him. But she had been like that for a long time.

Lois once told him it was because she lived so far away when the girls were smaller, but he had always thought there was more to it than that. Perhaps it was, as Lois said, that Kathleen felt she had to monopolize the girls' attention when she visited because she lived on the mainland and rarely saw them.

He had known Kathleen since they were both in kindergarten, but when Lois moved to town in high school, the two young women had become inseparable. So he had to concede that maybe his wife had known her better. That was why it had hurt Lois so much when Kathleen began to compete with her in high school, always trying to win at everything. And it was why it hurt Lois so much when their friendship ended. He could never forgive Kathleen for breaking his wife's heart.

"Amber's coming." Jade skidded into the kitchen in her stocking feet. "She's just getting dressed."

"Thanks, Jade. Now eat your breakfast." He poured another bowl for Amber and set it on the table with a spoon just as the girl plodded into the room and sat down, looking as exhausted as he felt.

"Good morning, sunshine," he said, chuckling when she looked up at him through bleary eyes. "Do you want juice or milk to drink?"

"Just water," said Amber, looking down at her lap while she ate. What was she doing?

"Amber doesn't like juice in the morning," Jade offered, digging her spoon into the bowl and taking a big bite.

"I see," said Roy, placing a glass of tap water in front of Amber and walking to the fridge for Nicole's instructions, surreptitiously looking over at Amber's lap to see the book there. Ah. They had warned him about this.

"Amber, you need to stop reading and finish up your breakfast so we can get going. We're late today."

The girl looked up at him, eyes wide at being caught. She quickly closed the book, whisked it under her leg where he couldn't see it, and looked at him with a meek expression on her face before picking up her spoon and taking a bite of cereal.

He laughed to himself. Kids were always trying to get away with things. The trick was to stay one step ahead of them. With Jade, it was easier. He knew her better.

Amber was more of a challenge. How did you get through to a kid that just wanted to read all the time?

The girls finished their breakfast in record time and went to grab their backpacks for school.

After dropping them off, Roy drove to meet Patrick for their morning run around the lake. They started slow, jogging side by side, which was fine by Roy. He was still tired, despite getting to bed early.

"How was your first day, Grandpa?"

"Argh, don't ask." He was still feeling the aches from his fall the previous evening, but he wouldn't tell Pat about that.

Pat laughed. "That bad, eh?"

"It was fine until last night, when Kathleen showed up and found me napping."

"Did she get mad?" Pat was chuckling now at his expense.

"Kathleen? No. She just managed around me, took over, had the kids help her make dinner, and then sat there smug at the other end of the table as if showing me how much they needed her."

"What's wrong with that? Is she a terrible cook or something?"

"No. She's an excellent cook. It was just the way she looked at me. Like she had come in and saved the day." He had to admit to himself that she *had* saved the day. He hated to think about what the girls could have got into if she hadn't come by when she did.

"Well, less work for you."

"Yeah, but I'm retired, and she worked all day. So the way she looked at me... Well, I got the impression she wanted me to feel guilty for napping or something."

"Probably all in your head. Any problems with the kids?"

"No, just that Amber seems to always be reading, and I can't get through to her. Thank goodness for Jade. She likes to do projects and spend time with me. Amber? Not a chance. She was like a fly to honey around Kathleen, though. Damned meddling woman."

"If I didn't know better, I'd think you were jealous."

"I'm not jealous." It was something else, more a sense that he was missing out on something. Kathleen had a full life, with her own business and charity work, and she still had time to connect with the girls. That connection with Amber seemed to come so easily to her.

The path narrowed, and Patrick pulled ahead so they could run single file, leaving Roy to his own thoughts. Roy thought back to the brief conversation he'd had with Jason the day before.

"Try to get Amber to take part in activities a bit more, Dad," Jason had said. "I've tried to get her to stop reading and do other things, but it's nearly impossible. Maybe you can get somewhere?"

"What's wrong with a kid wanting to read?"

"She's always reading. She would rather do that than anything. I just think she should get out more, be more active, more well-rounded."

"I'll try," said Roy, though over the past twenty-four hours he could see what his son was talking about. Amber never put her book down unless Kathleen was there, or the girls were doing chores.

They ran for the next half hour, and he tried to focus on the tree roots on the forest floor so he wouldn't trip, but thoughts of Kathleen intruded as he ran —like the look of triumph on her face the previous night when she looked at him from across the table. She'd worn that same look whenever she won something as a child or a teen. Back when they were friends.

He caught up with Patrick when the path widened so they could run side by side.

"Pat, have you talked to Kathleen much since she came back?"

Patrick slowed his pace. "No. I've seen her around town a few times, and I bought a present for my grandson at her store this past summer. She has a great selection of toys, you know. And modern ones too. This one was a set of blocks that he can make into a bunch of different cars, complete with an electric motor. Jackson loves it. He plays with it all the time."

"So she didn't keep in touch with you either? You know, after she left?"

"No, but I didn't really expect her to. She was Lois's friend, really. And when that fell apart, well, you know how it is. Besides, she went off to university in Vancouver, and I went out east. We all just grew apart."

"I thought you two had something going in high school."

Patrick laughed. "No. Kathleen and I were just friends."

Roy frowned, trying to remember where he got the impression Pat and Kat had been dating. He shook his head. Obviously, he'd misremembered.

"I guess I was wrong," he said. Still, he wished he could understand why they had grown apart. Why Kathleen had become so competitive, so opposed to Nicole and Justin's marriage, why she didn't speak to Lois until just before she died, and why she'd cut him out of her life like their friendship was a tumor to be removed.

"My advice: just start with what you have in front of you. Get along for the sake of the kids. A week will go by before you know it."

"Apparently they'll be away for closer to a month."

Patrick laughed out loud. "Well, good luck, my friend. You're going to need it."

The trail narrowed again, and Pat stepped up his pace and took off ahead, leaving Roy to wonder why he'd stayed friends with this guy for so long.

CHAPTER 5

When Kathleen arrived at her daughter's house that evening, she found Roy and the girls in the kitchen, eating stew he had made in the slow cooker.

"Want some?" he asked.

"That would be nice," she said, thinking she should taste it before committing to a whole bowl. "Don't get up, I'll get it." She opened the lid to the pot and ladled a small amount into a bowl. There were some buns in a box from the local bakery sitting on the counter, so she took one of those too and joined them at the table.

She took a tiny bite of the stew, aware that Roy was watching her. It was a bit bland and could have used more seasoning. She reached for the saltshaker and added some to the bowl, stirring it in and tasting it again. Now it was passable. She smiled up at him, trying to keep her face as neutral as possible for the sake of the children. He frowned a little and then looked toward Jade, who was telling them all about her day at school.

"The choir is singing 'I Want a Hippopotamus for Christmas' this year, and a song for Kwanzaa, and another one…" She looked up at Amber for help.

"The Huron Carol," said Amber.

"I love that song," said Kathleen. "It was one of my favorites when I was a girl."

"They had it that long ago, Nana?" asked Jade.

Roy laughed. "Yes, even that long ago!" he said. "We even had electricity back then," he added.

"But not computers. Right, Nana?" Amber asked.

"No, not computers."

"And no computer games?" Amber said. "What did you do for fun?"

Kathleen looked up to see Roy watching her again, enjoying this conversation.

"Well, this time of year, your grandfather and I would go out to skate if there was ice, or, on a snow day, we would go tobogganing."

"Or we would make things. I remember learning to redo furniture from my father when I was about your age," Roy said. "And I was a Boy Scout, so we used to go camping and fishing. Hiking."

Kathleen watched his face light up as he remembered their shared childhood. Before it all fell apart.

"In the summer we would go swimming," she said. "We spent so much time in the lake we always had prune fingers."

"And we had our instruments to practice," he said.

"What kind of instruments?" asked Amber.

"We played in the school band. I played drums, and your Nana here played the saxophone."

"What was it like?" asked Amber, looking up at Kathleen with interest. "I want to play in the band too."

Kathleen glanced at Roy, who was frowning, and then back to Amber. "Band was fun," she said. "I liked how each person has their own part, and, when they blend together, they can make something lovely. It isn't like playing alone. It's magic." She was wistful now, remembering the sounds of the music as it blended. "The percussionists—that's the drummers— keep the time, and the brass instruments give the whole sound depth. And then the wind instruments—the flute, the clarinet, the sax—they often take turns playing the melody. I think you would love it."

"Do you remember that band trip we took to Montreal, Kathleen?"

"Yes," she said, and she felt her face redden. Why would he bring up that trip?

"We were so excited," he told the kids. "We raised money for months and months to afford the plane fare for the whole band. We practiced over and over so we could play well at the festival there."

"It was the first time we had ever been on a plane. We were thirteen."

"Did you sit beside the window?"

"Your Nana did. I sat beside her in the middle because I was taller. And my friend Patrick—you know Pat—he was there too."

Kathleen watched his face as she told them about the plane ride, about getting to Montreal, about having to try to use their French lessons when they were billeted. He hadn't remembered the trip in the same detail.

There had been turbulence during the flight, and she remembered being so afraid they were going to crash. He had reached out to hold her hand, reassuring her that she would be fine. She could feel it now, that warm tingle of someone caring. Of Roy caring. After that, she never saw Roy the same way. In that instant, he had morphed from friend to boy and awakened her to new possibilities. She was tongue-tied around him for the rest of that trip until she realized nothing had changed for him. She was still just Kat, the friend he climbed trees with.

"What about Grandma? Was she in the band?" Jade interrupted her thoughts.

"Your Grandma didn't move to town until the following year," said Roy.

"And she didn't play in the band," Kathleen said.

"Did you know Grandma when she was young too?" Amber asked.

"I did," Kathleen said. She paused a moment, recalling how Lois had slipped in and draped herself around every crevice of her life. Within a few short weeks of meeting Lois, Kathleen had felt like she'd always been there. "Your grandma was one of my best friends when we were in high school."

Roy was solemn now, watching her as though he wanted to say something. She needed to change the subject before they got into more memories of Lois. She didn't want to remember how her best friend had betrayed her, and she certainly didn't want to go on about her virtues. Lois hadn't been all light and roses as Roy seemed to think. Even the dead had faults.

"Your Nana used to plug her ears when I practiced my sax and make excuses to go home," Kathleen said, trying to lighten her mood. "No, she didn't like band music at all. She always preferred to be in the water. She was on the swim team."

"I like to swim," said Amber. "Maybe I could be on a swim team."

"Maybe," Roy said.

"But Dad wants me to play sports. I hate sports."

"Swimming is a sport," said Kathleen, grateful they had shifted to another topic.

"Yeah, I guess so. But I think he means soccer. Dad and Jade like soccer."

"Maybe ask him if you can join the swim team after Christmas," she suggested.

"Yeah," said Jade. "You're a fast swimmer. You should try that."

"Tell you what," said Roy. "I'll look into the swimming team this week and find out what you need to know to join. Then I'll talk to your dad about it."

It's a good thing Lois was a swimmer, Kathleen thought. *If she had been a soccer player, he would be pushing Amber to try that.*

"Can you talk to him about the band, too?" Amber asked. "I want to learn to play the trombone. I like the way it looks."

Kathleen and Roy looked at each other, and Roy pulled a face, reminding her again of when they were younger. She had to look away quickly or she would have laughed out loud, thinking of all the wrong notes in store for Nicole and Jason.

"We can certainly ask your parents," Roy said, beaming.

Kathleen smiled along with him and then chided herself. How was it that this man, who had avoided her for decades, could still make her laugh? It was maddening.

He was maddening.

After dinner, Kathleen sent the girls off to finish their homework and stayed to help Roy with the dishes.

"That went well," she said. "It's been a while since Amber showed any interest in something other than her books."

"I hope Jason is okay with it."

"The swimming, or the trombone?" She chuckled.

"I think he'd like her to play a team sport," he said.

"Swimming's a good sport for Amber. She's an introvert, and she could compete against her own times, measure her progress. I think it would suit her.

Besides, it's a skill she can use for the rest of her life."

"And the trombone?" Roy laughed.

"Well, that may take a little getting used to, but she would be part of a group."

"And Jason can always escape to his workshop or the clinic if the noise is too much for him." He was laughing harder now.

"Maybe they can build a soundproof room," Kathleen said, laughing along with him.

"That's the ticket," said Roy, putting the slow cooker away and wiping down the counter. "Well, that's that. What would you like to do now?"

His words reminded her of the work she had been pushing to the back of her mind.

"I need to track down a new supplier, follow up on some orders that didn't get here, and revise the plans for my Christmas tree. I'm entering the festival this year. Apparently, it's a community tradition that the toy store missed out on when the previous owner lost his wife. I guess it had been her thing, and he just couldn't face it." She looked at Roy's suddenly haunted eyes and cringed inwardly. He had just lost his wife, and here she was, talking about a widower. She needed to steer away from talk of widows and widowers if she were going to keep her promise to Nicole. "Anyway, it would be good exposure for the store, and it helps the kids. A win-win, really."

He stared at her, his face void of expression again. The warmth between them was gone, the ice wall between them re-freezing. What could she say to bring back his smile? She had always liked his smile.

"Have you ever been to the Community Tree Festival?" He had to answer a direct question, didn't he?

"That fundraiser for the children's development center? No. I think Lois used to take Jason when he was little, though."

"You didn't go too?" *Why am I asking a question he already answered?*

"No, I was working. I missed a lot of Jason's growing up because of work."

Kathleen knew Lois had never worked after they married, devoting all her time to Roy and Jason. Maybe that was why her pies were always flaky and perfect. Kathleen fished around for something else to say to move the conversation away from Lois.

"Well, you can go this year. The girls will enjoy it. There are crafts and face painting, and of course they can see the trees and have some hot chocolate."

"And it would get Amber away from those books for a few hours," said Roy, nodding slowly. *Is that agreement?* She would take it as agreement.

"Here." She rushed over to the calendar on the fridge before he found a reason to change his mind. "I'll put it on Nicole's list." She marked it on the calendar and circled it with a big heart. "Oh, and while I'm here, I thought I could add the Christmas sailpast next week. You can see the lights from my condo, and the girls really enjoyed it last year." She turned to find him looking at her with a puzzled expression.

"What's wrong?" she asked, looking up at him. He had walked over to the fridge to watch her.

"Nothing." His eyes were inscrutable, his face again void of expression. Why were men so hard to read?

"Would you like to see the sailpast from my condo?" she asked. "I live downtown near the harbor."

"Why don't you put it on the calendar for the girls? I can find something else to do that night. Pat has been after me the past few days to go to the pub with him."

She felt the disappointment as though it were a blow to her chest. Though they had shared memories of a better time, a time when they had been friends, Roy was right. Too much had passed since. She meant nothing to him. He meant nothing to her. She needed to remember that.

So why was she feeling so overwhelmingly sad?

She looked at him a moment longer, willing her voice not to shake, then broke their gaze and said, "I should get going." She walked toward the kitchen door, then paused and turned around in time to see that he had been watching her cross the room. "Unless you need me for anything else tonight?"

"No." He shook his head and pushed himself away from the counter. "I'll just make sure they've finished their homework and get an early night."

"Good night, then." She climbed the stairs to say good night to the girls and then left for home.

As she drove, she thought of the easy conversation and memories they'd shared. It had been a nice evening until the kids left. Then he had changed, and it had become awkward. He had inserted Lois into the conversation more times than she was comfortable with. Even dead, Lois was still the center of everyone's attention. She shook her head, chiding herself. How could she even think that? Lois had fallen hard for Roy, wanted him, and won him. They'd had, by all accounts, a good marriage. She needed to stop comparing herself to Lois—and stop comparing her failed marriage to their successful one.

She needed to move on and stop dredging up old memories of when she and Roy had been close. She had work to do. Grandchildren to care for. She would get along as Nicole had asked her, and that was all. She and Roy would never be more than acquaintances who happened to be related through their children's marriage. Roy had chosen Lois.

CHAPTER 6

"Grandpa, can we get a tree?" Jade asked when they were eating breakfast.

He looked up to see two pairs of eyes watching him for his response.

"Sure, that's a great idea."

"And can Nana come?" asked Amber.

He tried not to scowl. He had learned to tolerate her coming over at dinnertime, had even had a reasonably good conversation the last time—though why she was so crabby when she mentioned the band trip they took to Montreal, he had no idea. He remembered it being fun.

"I think Nana is too busy at the store this time of year to take a weekend morning to get a tree." And it had to be the morning. It would likely be an all-day event, and he didn't want to be decorating the thing long into the night.

"Can you ask her? Pleeease," said Jade.

"Please. Please. Please," said Amber. "Nana might even make cookies with us."

Cookies. He had to admit he did like cookies, though they always reminded him of Lois. She had always baked cookies this time of year. She had been the one to decorate the tree too. Maybe he should ask Kathleen to help. She could take over that part. He wouldn't have to do more than put on the lights. Then maybe he could leave them alone for a few hours, watch a hockey game with Pat at the pub, and forget about the tree and the cookies—and the huge gap in his life—for an hour or two. The more he thought about it, the better the idea sounded. He would ask Kathleen, and he hoped she said yes.

That evening, Roy was sitting in the living room, watching the sports highlights, and waiting for the casserole in the oven to cook when Kathleen walked into the house.

"Hey," he said. "You're early." *Do I sound upbeat and casual enough?*

"Jackie and one of my temporary staff have it covered for now. I'll go back at eight to relieve her and cash out."

"Come sit down. Take a load off until dinner's ready. The girls are playing upstairs."

She eyed him suspiciously and came into the room where he could get a better look at her. She wore business attire as usual. Not a suit, but what they called business casual: slacks, a jacket, and a white blouse. She looked nice, though Kathleen had always been careful about her appearance. When they were younger, Lois had joked about Kathleen's signature haircut: a blunt bob —now streaked liberally with silver— that she wore like a helmet.

That, and the frown on her face, told him she was ready for battle. He needed to play this carefully.

"Do you have a lot of temporary staff?" he asked, hoping that she would say yes. If she thought he had deliberately left this request to the last minute so she couldn't participate, this whole thing would backfire.

"I have one key person I count on, and a woman who helps me part-time while her kids are in school. Oh, and a couple of high-school students work for me on the weekends and after school. They're mature and very dependable."

"Well, I was thinking—actually, the girls were asking—if we could... set up a Christmas tree tomorrow."

"Do you know where they keep it?"

"They usually get a live one, so I thought we could go to the Christmas tree farm just outside of town and get one tomorrow."

"I'm sure the girls will enjoy that." She had that mutinous look on her face again. The one she used to use whenever she caught a whiff of injustice. He had to fix this before it went sideways. He had made a promise to Jason and Nicole and the girls.

"Do you have someone who can cover for you at the store tomorrow morning?"

"You mean you want me to come too?" She was smiling. That was a good sign.

"I wouldn't want to choose a tree without you," he said lightly, though he was already considering how badly this outing could go. "You were really helpful that year Lois's father died, and we went out to get the tree for them. Remember?"

Her face changed from pleasure to— what? Pain? Why had he brought up Lois's father dying? He needed to stop that. It probably brought up painful memories of Kathleen's own father, who had left to live with another woman only a few months before they graduated. According to Lois, Kathleen's parents' divorce had been devastating for her. It was one reason Kathleen left town right after high school and rarely visited, especially after her mother remarried and took on her new husband's children. As Lois had said, "I just lost my father. She lost her whole family."

He looked across at Kathleen, who was now consulting her phone. He remembered the day she'd learned of her father's affair. It had been raining, and he'd found her at the park, sitting with Patrick at a table under one of the picnic shelters. Pat had left shortly after he arrived, saying he had to get home for dinner or his mother would be worried. Roy had taken Pat's place and pulled Kat close to him, kissing her on the forehead and telling her it would all be okay. She had leaned into him, tiny and sad, and sobbed. That was why he had kissed her that night. To keep her from being so very sad. And it had worked. She had perked up, and she and he and Lois, and sometimes Pat, had spent the next few months enjoying the last year of high school.

Until Lois's father died. Was that when things had all changed between them?

Kathleen looked up from her phone and turned toward him. "I can probably help get the tree in the morning," she said, "after I get the store opened, and then come back after five to help decorate. Would that work?"

She was rearranging her schedule. *Good.* He'd take what he could get. He pasted a smile on his face and tried to sound grateful. "That would be great. Do you have time next weekend to come as well? I want to put up the lights, but I need someone to stay with the girls while I do it."

She glanced at the phone again, scrolled through something on the screen with her finger, then nodded. "I can take off most of next Saturday. My staff want as many hours as they can get this month."

"Great." She could help. "The girls would also love to make cookies with you."

She beamed at him. "Oh, I haven't made cookies with children in... well... since Nicole was small."

"Are you sure? The girls used to love making cookies with Lois."

Her face was pinched again.

"What did I say this time?" This woman was so confusing.

"They made cookies with Lois." She sighed as though talking to a child. "And that meant that they didn't want to make them with me."

"Oh." That was all he could say, though he was mentally defending his wife. He finally had to say it out loud. "She was here, and you weren't. It wasn't a contest."

"No," she mumbled so low he could barely make it out. "No contest because she already won."

A faint beep sounded from the kitchen.

"Is that a timer?" she asked.

"What? Oh, yes, the food is ready." He stopped trying to puzzle her out and pulled his thoughts back to the task at hand. "Let's get the girls and have supper."

At dinner, they told the girls they would take them to get a Christmas tree. Jade whooped with excitement, and Amber smiled.

"And Amber, I found out about the swim team," Roy said. "We'll ask your parents next time they call."

It was Amber's turn to whoop.

Roy looked around the table and took another bite of his food, realizing that this was perhaps the first time he had felt content around a table since Lois had passed. She had been right to encourage him to spend time with the children, but it was more than that. He took another bite of the casserole and looked up at Kathleen, who quickly cast her eyes downward. It was nice to have the civil Kathleen back in his life instead of the sparring partner. He hadn't realized how much he had missed her.

"Nana," said Amber, "can we do Christmas baking too?"

"Yeah," said Jade. "We can help. We're good at baking."

Kathleen looked from one to the other and then up at him. He nodded in encouragement.

"If memory serves, you make a pretty mean rum ball," he said.

"Just remember to leave some rum for the cookies this time, Roy."

Her tone was serious, but when he looked more closely, he saw a hit of humor in her eyes. He laughed at the memory of the first and last time he got sick on alcohol. They had been making rum balls at her house the Christmas before graduation, trying to cheer up Lois, who had lost her father only a few weeks earlier. It had been a good night except for the getting sick part, and it was the last time he remembered the three of them having so much fun.

Tonight felt a little like that night.

He looked up at Kathleen again and considered her carefully. She had aged—who hadn't?—and she didn't resemble Kat, the girl with whom he had climbed trees, gone skiing, and raced from the beach to the floating dock in the middle of the local lake.

Sometime over the years, Kat had changed into this stranger named Kathleen. A stranger who, until this week, he hadn't wished to get to know at all. Until this week, he hadn't considered they could find enough common ground to do more than tolerate each other, much less rekindle their old friendship. But this week had changed things. She had softened toward him. They had shared old memories. Laughed.

Lois would be pleased.

CHAPTER 7

Kathleen woke, excited about the day ahead.

It had been years since she had been to a Christmas tree farm to hunt for just the right tree. Chris hadn't liked the fuss of going out every year, so early in their marriage they had agreed on an artificial one, upgrading as soon as she could for the type that was already strung with lights. It made things easier, he said. In reality, it was easier.

Easier for her to set up the tree on her own.

That same artificial tree was now in her storage locker. Perhaps she would pull it out in the next few days.

Or not.

Maybe she could just make do with the tree at Nicole's house this year. It would be less work, and she could avoid the painful process of pulling out ornaments she had collected over the years. They just reminded her of what she had lost: her son, her home, her husband. Her family.

This way of thinking wasn't getting her anywhere. She still had Nicole and her granddaughters, and if she could continue to get along with Roy, she would be invited to spend more time with them. She thought about Roy for a moment. He had been holding up his end of their promise to Nicole. He had even been pleasant—perhaps even fun —to be with. It reminded her of their old friendship. Before everything changed between them.

"No," she said out loud, pushing the negative memories to the far corner of her mind. Today, she would keep the unpleasant memories to a minimum and focus instead on making a new batch of memories with her grandchildren. And maybe help Roy to do the same, though that seemed an impossible task. Hearing Lois's name every time he opened his mouth was grating on her. She didn't need the constant reminder of how much better Lois was, how talented she was, how much more she was loved.

"Stop." She was doing it again. She needed to remember the technique her friend Sandy had taught her when Chris left. Stop the negative thoughts, examine them, and then reframe them. Lois was talented and loved, but that didn't have anything to do with Katheen's worth. And Kathleen knew she shouldn't compare herself to Lois. Especially now that Lois was dead. No one could win against a ghost.

An hour later, Kathleen greeted Casey and Josh and went through the schedule and instructions they needed to follow while she was away for the day.

"I know you two can handle things, but if something comes up, I'm only a phone call away. Here's my cell number again in case you need anything. I'm going to get a Christmas tree."

"Can I help decorate it?" Casey asked, and Kathleen looked at her blankly for a moment. Then she looked around the room. The snowflakes that Jackie had made from one of the craft books were hanging from the ceiling, and there were a few lights along the top shelf, but the decorations still needed help. Why hadn't she remembered she still needed a tree for the store? And what else had she been forgetting in the last few days?

She still needed a tree for the festival too, but decorating three trees in a few days seemed daunting. She thought for a moment and remembered the artificial tree in her storage locker. She could put the live tree here in the store and advertise the festival for a few days. When it was time to move it to the community center, she could bring in her old artificial tree to replace it.

Turning to Casey, she said, "Yes, of course. We'll set it up in the window." She pointed to the location. "And we can set up a train track that goes around it at the base."

"I used to have a train set," Josh said. "Can I help with that?"

"You can," Kathleen said, pleased with their enthusiasm. They wanted to help, and, knowing their other talents, she was sure they would do a great job. She wouldn't have to decorate alone this year. It was a refreshing change and maybe another way to make new memories of the season.

"There's an open train set in the back. The last owner used to set it up along the top shelf every year. It's on the last row of shelving in a box marked *Christmas*. I'll bring the tree in around two, and you can take turns decorating it while I look after the customers this afternoon. And, Casey, can you check to see if we got more of those craft boxes in?" She pointed to the last box on the top shelf— a craft set for making tree ornaments. "I ordered them a couple of weeks ago, but I don't know if they've arrived yet. Meanwhile, I want you to open one up and use that to make the ornaments for the tree. It will be a dry run for the festival tree we need to decorate next week."

She left them discussing plans for the tree and walked to the office. There was definitely something she was missing. Her desk was as she'd left it, and she sat down in the hope that being in the same place she worked every day would remind her. But nothing came to mind.

She pulled her planning spreadsheet up on her computer and went over the list of tasks, updating the list as she went until she found it: the order she had been waiting for hadn't been put in. She had messed up. She had been so distracted this past month with marketing and planning that she had missed the deadline to order toys that would land in her store before December first. She needed to get in touch with her suppliers immediately and track down any stock that could be delivered to the island before the first week of December was done.

How could she have been so stupid? This would mean overhauling her newsletters and changing her marketing campaigns to focus on another toy. And her Christmas tree entry? That would need to be redone as well. She started a list of suppliers she had used before and decided to start by calling the first on the list right away. Her main supplier had been helpful when she was getting started in the business. Hopefully they would have something she could order. She sighed as she dialed and waited while the automatic voice system cheerfully put her on hold. This would take all day.

She was jotting down the other names and phone numbers and listening to Christmas carols through the telephone receiver when she was startled by the alarm on her watch—the alarm she had set to remind her to leave and meet the girls. The alarm she had set to remind herself that family was more important than business. Reluctantly, she hung up the phone, folded up the list she'd made, and put it in her pocket. She could make phone calls while they were waiting for cookies to bake. Or she could slip into the bathroom when the kids were busy with Roy, maybe? The second alarm sounded. She had to leave right away, or she would be late.

She drove to the house, faster than she normally would, to find a pair of excited girls waiting for her in the foyer.

"We thought you'd never get here," said Jade, jumping up from the bottom step where she'd been sitting. "Come on, Nana!"

Feeling guilty for making them wait, she followed them to Roy's truck and climbed in the front next to a silent Roy. He wore a disapproving frown while the girls piled into the seat behind. She could just imagine what he was thinking.

Lois never would have kept him or the children waiting.

"We want to get there early so we get the best one!" said Amber.

"The good thing about a tree farm," said Roy, "is that there are a lot of best ones to choose from." He glared over at Kathleen. "Ready?"

"Ready," she said. "Oh, and I need to get one for the store while we're there. So I'll need help to choose it."

"We'll help!" said Jade.

"I was hoping you would say that." She had to stay calm and remember that the tree was one of the tasks she had to get done. The calls could wait an hour or two.

She hoped.

They arrived at the tree farm at eleven, amid a buzz of excitement from other shoppers searching for their perfect tree. The girls leapt from the truck.

"We need a saw before we go," said Roy. "The U-Cut trees are down that gravel path there." He pointed to the path lit by lights and wreaths.

"Can we run ahead?" asked Jade.

"Only if you don't go too far," said Roy, staying his hand when Kathleen tried to protest. "They'll be fine," he said to her. "They need a little independence at this age, and it's a pretty safe space."

He walked over to a kiosk where a worker was signing out handsaws, and she watched the girls scamper down the path, trying to stay calm. He was back only a few short moments later, and she breathed a little easier when she saw the girls a few yards ahead. They were walking around several trees, arguing their merits with one another.

"This'll keep them occupied for a bit," said Roy, waving his hand in their direction.

"Hopefully they'll wear themselves out by bedtime. These girls have more energy than I ever remember having," said Kathleen.

"Oh, I remember it a bit differently." Roy smiled. "Young Jade there reminds me of what you were like at that age."

"Really?"

"You were always game to try anything and everything."

"Perhaps," she said, considering it. "I've always been interested in adventure, that's true."

"Have you had a lot of adventures in your life?" he asked.

"Well, Chris and I backpacked around Europe for a few months the year before Nicole was born, and we took trips to Mexico and Hawaii when the children were growing up. But then his career took off, and he began traveling alone for conferences while I stayed home to raise the kids."

"It's too bad you didn't keep traveling if you loved it so much."

"When you have little kids, someone has to be their stability." Besides, Chris hadn't wanted her to travel with him. She found out later that he had been more interested in traveling with a new, no-strings-attached companion every few months. Until Jolene finally nabbed him and held on.

Kathleen supposed she should be grateful to her. If Jolene hadn't come along, Kathleen might still be in a loveless marriage. She just wished Jolene had come along earlier so she hadn't wasted so many years in denial. Maybe she would even have found a new partner by now. One she could trust. Though she doubted it. Men had a habit of leaving and letting her down.

"Do you travel much?" she asked, banishing the memories again.

"No, I haven't had a lot of opportunity. I was running the hospital for a long time, and then when Lois got sick, I nursed her. We did a few family vacations, of course, but usually it was Lois, and before that my parents, who took Jason on vacation."

She sighed inwardly at the mention of Lois but tamped down her frustration long enough to ask, "Was she sick long?"

"Yes. On and off since she was diagnosed fifteen years ago."

"Fifteen years?" How had she not known this?

"She was first diagnosed when Jason was about sixteen. It went into remission a few years later, and we thought she'd beat it. But it came back, and this time she couldn't win."

"I'm sorry."

"Well, at least she got to see Jason grow up, and she got to meet her granddaughters."

Kathleen couldn't speak, thinking about her former friend. Why hadn't she known about Lois's long battle with cancer? Nicole must have mentioned it. But maybe she just hadn't paid attention. And, if she were honest with herself, knowing might not have mattered. She and Lois had broken ties. Indeed, they never would have met again were it not for their children getting to know each other when Nicole visited her grandmother, who still lived next to Roy's mother.

She thought back to the day she'd learned Nicole was destined to move to Sunshine Bay. She had been in the kitchen chopping vegetables to add to the steamer when Nicole had flown into the house, shouting "Mom!" and letting the screen door bang shut behind her.

"How was your visit with Nana?" Kathleen asked as she transferred the cut-up carrots to the steamer and returned to the chopping board to slice up some zucchini.

"Oh, Mom! It was perfect. Jason asked me to marry him!" She thrust her left hand forward, startling Kathleen into looking up at the new ring glinting in the sunlight.

"Ouch!" Kathleen yowled when her knife failed to find purchase on the smooth zucchini skin and instead sliced along the back of her thumb. She dropped the knife onto the counter and grabbed a nearby tea towel to staunch the blood dripping on her newly cut vegetables.

"Oh, no! I'm so sorry. Are you okay? Let me get a bandage." Nicole ran to retrieve the first aid kit from the kitchen cupboard and ushered Kathleen to a nearby chair. "Sit down. Let me look at it."

Kathleen sat, unsure if her daze was from the sudden bite of the knife or the realization that she would now be tied to Lois and Roy's son for life. Jason was a nice boy. She had no concern there. But he looked so much like Roy when he was younger. So much like the boy she had loved.

Nicole had carefully removed the cloth and examined the cut. "This is going to need stitches," she said. "Come on. I'm taking you into emergency." She pulled

Kathleen up from her chair after putting the tea towel back on the wound and ran to turn off the oven and stove.

They'd arrived at the hospital, and Nicole took charge. Kathleen watched, detached, as her daughter guided her to the front desk to check in, led her down to the bed in the emergency room, and finally conferred on her behalf with a doctor who wasn't much older than Nicole. Her baby had grown up. Her baby was getting married. Her baby didn't need her anymore.

She slumped against the back of the chair. *I'm superfluous*, she thought, staring at her hand. It lay on a tray between her and the doctor as though detached from her body. The doctor's calm voice kept her in a semi-trance as he described what he would do, and she barely felt the poke of a needle injecting a local anesthetic. He was quick about the sutures—ten stitches, a lot more than she'd thought it would take. This cut had been bad, but in hindsight not as bad as learning that Nicole would join Roy's family. The family that, because of Lois, she would never be part of. That was the deepest cut of all.

How will I ever cope?

But she had coped. After planning the wedding and seeing her daughter and son-in-law off to complete their residency in Ontario, she volunteered for every committee she could find. Keeping busy helped her avoid missing her daughter—and avoid the reality that Terrence, her son, had little time for her. Now that he was going daily to university, their relationship had been reduced to notes exchanged on the fridge whiteboard. She posted questions or basic information for him, like "dinner's in the fridge" or "what time will you be home?" and he scribbled a quick "thanks" or a "don't wait up" in reply. When he finally flew off to Ontario to pursue his own medical career, they had reduced their relationship to text messages every few days. At least she had that with Terrence. With Chris it was worse. Volunteering helped her avoid the truth that she was the only person left in her marriage. Chris had checked out years ago. She had just refused to see it.

Would she have felt differently about Lois if she had known about the cancer then? She shook her head in answer to her own question. Probably not. She would have assumed Lois would win against cancer, just as she won all her battles. Lois had a way of winning everything she tried—swimming races, the solo spot in the school choir concert, track and field events—and Kathleen had always come up second-best. And Lois smushed her face in her failure in that subtle way only teenaged girls could.

Kathleen had assumed that Lois would do what Lois always did: land on her feet and keep moving forward.

Not this time, though. Lois had lost the last battle, and Kathleen had only known about the last few months of her suffering, when she had come to help with the girls while Nicole worked and Jason and Roy nursed Lois.

She should have paid closer attention. Nicole had needed her far more than she'd realized, and she had chosen fundraising committees over her daughter. Was she doing the same thing with her business? The list of suppliers burned in her pocket, coaxing her to find time to make the calls, but she was soon distracted by the sound of feet running toward them.

"Nana, Grandpa!" The girls stopped in front of them, panting from exertion. "We've found the best trees." Each girl grabbed a hand of a grandparent and pulled them along.

"Okay, okay. Slow down," Kathleen said, laughing at their excitement. "Let's see what you've found."

They walked down the path, and the girls showed them their prizes. "This noble fir will be perfect for the store," she said, and Amber beamed.

"That was my favorite! I like the bluish-green needles."

"And it's perfect for heavy ornaments. Some of the ornaments at the store may be the larger than normal." Of course, she still had to confirm the theme. She needed to get back to the store soon.

"I like this one best," Jade said, pulling them down the path to a stand of Fraser fir trees. "It looks silver."

"It does! I think your mom and dad will like it too," said Kathleen.

"Sounds like we have two winners," said Roy. "And two girls to help me cut them down."

Kathleen flagged down the attendant standing nearby to ask for some tree netting. The attendant produced tags for the trees they could take to the cashier, and, once the first tree fell, she showed them how to wrap it. When they felled the second tree, the girls scrambled to wrap it themselves with only a little help from Roy.

"We did it!" said the twins, excited at their accomplishment.

Kathleen laughed and stood back, snapping a picture of the trio with her cell phone to share later with Nicole and Jason.

"Now let's get these trees to the truck. And then I think there's some hot chocolate at the café near the entrance."

"Yeah!" The girls ran ahead while the attendant and Roy each hoisted a tree and Kathleen went ahead to pay.

When they were done, they dropped one tree at home, and then Kathleen drove her car to the store while Roy and the girls followed in the truck.

"Thanks so much," she said when they arrived. "I have a few hours of work here, but I'll be back to help with the decorating this evening. Jackie's able to close up tonight."

"Let me give you a hand setting it up before I go." Roy hoisted the tree out of the truck and carried it inside. The girls followed and made a beeline to the back of the store, where she had set up stations where children could test out the interlocking blocks and a few games. Kathleen found that the longer she kept kids in the store, the more likely their parents or grandparents were to buy something.

Roy worked with Josh to set up the tree in the window using an old stand Josh had found in the back room. "There, I think that's straight now," he finally said, stepping back to admire their handiwork.

"Perfect," she said, pleased with the way the tree fit in the window. "Now all we need are some decorations."

"On it," said Josh. He and Casey opened the box they had found in the back and pulled out a string of lights.

"I'll leave you to it, then," Kathleen said, and turned to thank Roy again for his help. Her daughter would have been proud of the way they were getting along.

"You're welcome," he said, looking around the room. "You've done a lot of work in here. It looks completely different than it did a few years ago."

"New management, new store," she said. "It's been a lot of work but also quite rewarding. Especially when I see children learning and enjoying the toys."

"Well, it looks great. I'm going to have some work tearing that pair away from the blocks." He tilted his head in the direction of the girls.

"They must have building blocks at home."

"Probably." He turned toward her. "Hey, do you like pizza?"

"Love it. It's been years, but..."

"Well, my friend Nick Romano makes a great one. I'll order it for about six thirty?"

"I'll be there," she said before turning to greet a customer coming through the door.

Roy went to gather the girls and usher them outside.

"Bye, Nana! See you soon!"

She stood at the window and waved, feeling a little guilty for sending them off with Roy. They had both consumed candy canes with their hot chocolate and were likely on a sugar high.

But she had work to do, and he was a big boy. He could take care of himself.

CHAPTER 8

Roy drove two excited girls home, only
half listening to their chatter while he
concentrated on the road in front of him
and went over the day's events in his
mind. Kathleen had been tense when
she arrived late that morning, like she
wished to be somewhere else. Did he
make her as uncomfortable as she
made him?

"Grandpa, can we get a hamburger for
lunch?" Jade pointed at the fast-food

restaurant on the road ahead of them. "Dad takes us there sometimes."

"Not a bad idea," he said, signalling to move the car into the right lane and then merging into the drive-through lane. "Let's get our meals to go and take them home."

Sitting around the kitchen table a half hour later, he was glad they had gone for fast food. Fatigue was overtaking him, and he didn't have the energy to cook.

"When will Nana be here?" Amber asked. "When can we start decorating the tree?"

"She'll be here about six thirty," he said, and wondered not for the first time how Kathleen always managed to look so fresh and upbeat after working all day. It was obvious that she worked hard. Her store was well-run and tidy, and he had enjoyed visiting her realm. Her staff seemed to like her too. It was as though the Kathleen Lois had always talked about in hushed, warning tones wasn't there anymore. Instead, there was a vibrant woman who he wanted to get to know better. A warm feeling flooded him as he realized Kathleen was a woman he admired. What was that about? She was so different from Lois. Less concerned with always making things perfect at home. Less concerned with how others were living. He hadn't heard one word of gossip since he'd been spending time with her.

Maybe the old competitive Kat was gone.

"What can we do while we wait for her?" asked Jade around a mouthful of french fries.

Roy turned to consider her question. He would have to think about Kathleen later.

"We can set up the tree and put on the lights. Then maybe you two can play until Nana gets here."

They cleared up the kitchen and spent the next hour untangling lights, testing each string to make sure they were ready to hang. He then got them to help with the outside light strings so the following week his task would be easier.

After an hour, the kids were done.

"Grandpa, can we go play for a while now?" Jade wheedled. "Maybe help you put the lights on the tree later?"

He looked from one face to another and recognized the longing to be elsewhere.

He had to admit that putting lights on trees was not the most exciting task.

"You two go on. I'll put the lights on. You can help put the ornaments on when Nana gets here."

He watched them bounce upstairs and turned toward the tree and the neat pile of lights beside it. Then he turned his attention to the couch.

He could sit down for a few minutes to look at the sports highlights before he got started. He had a few hours left until Kat got here. *Kat.* When had he started thinking of her as Kat again? He flipped on the television sports channel but only watched a few highlights before he drifted off to sleep.

CHAPTER 9

Kathleen covered the till while Casey turned her artistic talents to painting the display window with snowflakes. Josh assembled the old train set, running the tracks along the edge of the window display and around the tree that was perfuming the shop with the scents of pine and forest walks.

They decorated the tree using glass balls Jackie had made from a kit during the slow times, and with other ornaments found in the back. By the time Jackie arrived, they were done, and Kathleen stepped outside to greet her and to admire their sparkling, Christmassy window and the little train click-clacking its way along the tracks.

"What do you think?" she asked Jackie.

"It looks fantastic," Jackie said. "Look at how all the snowflakes are unique. It looks like the train is traveling through a winter wonderland!"

They stepped inside and heaped praise on the pair for their great work.

"And did you see we put the puzzles you advertised in this week's newsletter among the presents?" asked Josh. "Hopefully it will help push them."

"You're going to be perfect for that business school you're planning to attend next year," said Kathleen. "You have an instinct."

Josh smiled at the praise. "See where Casey put Trixie Turtle?" He pointed to the stuffed animal playing a xylophone. "That should amuse the kids."

"It's perfect." She looked from one to the other. "Thank you both. We're now officially ready for the holiday season. Great job."

They grinned and shared a high five before Josh headed to the back of the store to grab his belongings.

"Casey," Kathleen said, "did you have time to check the back for those extra craft kits I ordered? "

"I couldn't see them, Kathleen. Sorry. Jackie, do you know where they are?"

"I can't recall any coming in, but I'll check tonight after Josh gets back from his break. Now off you two go," she said, and shooed Kathleen and Casey out the door.

As she left, Kathleen glanced again at the inviting window display. This would be a good month for revenue. She could feel it. By January, if things went as planned, she could finally say she had turned a profit.

Now she just needed to continue engaging with the community so they got to know the store for what it was: a place to find materials so kids could be creative and learn new skills. One way to do that was to enter the Tree Festival with a tree that was memorable and that would, as Josh suggested, encourage shoppers to visit her store all year round.

When she arrived at her daughter's house at six thirty after stopping to get some baking supplies from the supermarket, she found the pizza delivery girl about to ring the doorbell.

"Here, how much do I owe you?" she asked, setting her cloth grocery bag down on the porch.

She paid for the pizzas and carried the food inside to a quiet house—quiet except for the snoring coming from the living room and the faint dance music coming from upstairs.

Setting the pizzas and groceries down on the table in the hallway, she walked over to Roy, who was again asleep on the couch. She shook him. "Roy, the pizza's here."

There was no response, so she shook him a little harder and spoke a little louder. "Roy, the pizza's here."

Still, he snored on, a faltering snore that stopped and started. It reminded her of a car engine that stuttered the first few times she turned the key and then leapt to life, putting along until it faltered again.

She leaned over and shouted near his ear. "Roy!"

"Whaa—?" He opened his eyes and shot up, trying to find his bearings. "Oh, it's you. You scared me."

"Roy, where are the kids?"

"Upstairs doing their homework."

"Roy, aren't you getting enough rest? This is the second time in a week I've found you asleep on the couch."

"I'm fine."

"No, I don't think you are. You need to see a doctor and find out what's going on. You can't be falling asleep at five every evening."

"Yeah, fine. I'll go see a doctor, okay?"

"Tomorrow?"

He scowled at her. "Fine. I'll make an appointment. Happy now?"

"Just make sure you do," she said. "I don't want the girls to actually set the house on fire next time."

His face reddened. Good. *He should be ashamed*, she thought. "Now get up. The pizza's here. I'll go get the girls, and you can take the pizza to the kitchen."

"Okay." He sat for a few more seconds as though finding the strength to get up. What was wrong with the man? He looked exhausted.

She climbed the stairs and knocked on the bedroom doors across the hall from each other. "Girls, pizza's here."

Jade bounced into the hallway. "Hi, Nana!"

"Go wash your hands and then go to the kitchen. Grandpa is getting out the plates."

She knocked on Amber's door again. There was no answer, so she opened it to find her asleep on the bed. Maybe she had been too hard on Roy. If even Amber needed a nap after the day's activities, there was no reason a grown man shouldn't. Still, he had been hard to awaken, and she was sure he had stopped breathing for a moment. He needed to get himself checked out, just to be on the safe side.

"Amber." She shook her granddaughter's arm. "Pizza's here."

Amber opened her eyes and closed them again. "Amber? Are you okay?"

She opened her eyes again and nodded. "Yes, Nana. Just needed a bit of a rest."

"Aren't you sleeping?"

"Uh-huh…" The girl's eyes fluttered shut again.

"Amber, wake up."

"Jus… a… minute…" the girl mumbled.

This wasn't good. This wasn't good at all. She would have to ask Roy what time he was getting the girls off to bed. Their mother had strict rules about bedtime at eight thirty. Nicole believed in a good night's sleep.

She left Amber sleeping and went downstairs to join the others.

"What's going on with Amber? I can't get her to wake up. She looks exhausted."

"I dunno," Jade said, a little too quickly.

"What don't you know?"

"What Amber is doing at night."

Kathleen looked up at Roy, who turned toward Jade.

"Is she reading after dark again? I told her not to do that."

Jade's eyes widened. "No. She wouldn't. She..."

"What do you think she's doing at night?" Kathleen asked.

"I can't say."

"Can't say or won't say?" asked Roy. His voice was rising.

"I promised..." said Jade, shoving the last bite of her pizza slice into her mouth. "Can I be excused?" she asked through a mouthful of food.

"Yes," said Kathleen.

"No," said Roy, who narrowed his eyes at Kathleen. "I want you to tell me what's going on. Is there something going on with Amber?"

Jade shook her head. "No. Everything's fine. Thanks, Nana." She took her plate to the dishwasher and fled the room.

"Why did you excuse her?" Roy said. "She would have said something."

"I think it's best to ask Amber. I'll go upstairs and see if I can get her to wake up."

She left a half-eaten slice of pizza on her plate, climbed the stairs again, and stood outside Amber's door. There were voices inside that stopped when she knocked, so she pushed it open to find the two girls together. She could tell by the guilty look on Amber's face that Jade had warned her.

"Amber, It's time for dinner. Come on."

"Yes, Nana." Amber feigned scratching her leg, avoiding her grandmother's eyes.

"It's Hawaiian pizza." Jade said. "It's your favorite kind."

She looked up and smiled tentatively. "Okay. I'm coming."

"And Jade, after dinner we have a tree to decorate, so come back down in about ten minutes, okay?"

"Yes, Nana."

Back in the kitchen, Roy was still sitting at the table where she'd left him.

"Did you find out what it is? Why she's so tired?"

"No, but maybe we need to monitor her for a few days." She sat back down to finish the pizza on her plate. "This is good," she said as Amber came into the room and sat down, biting hungrily into the piece her grandfather passed her.

Probably filling her mouth so she can't answer questions, thought Kathleen. Her granddaughters were quick thinkers.

She turned her attention to Roy, who was watching Amber eat with concern on his face, and changed the subject.

"Well, you've got the tree in the tree stand. How long will it take to put on the lights?" Though why he hadn't already started on that was beyond her imagination. What had they been doing all day?

He frowned at the unexpected change in conversation and thought for a moment before answering. "Probably forty-five minutes, maybe an hour. Depends on how many strings we have to test for burnt bulbs."

"And you found the decorations okay?" she continued, watching Amber busily filling her mouth with pizza and throwing furtive glances at her grandparents.

"They were right where Jason said they were."

"Have you spoken to Jason since they landed?"

"Not since that first day, but I'm sure they're busy. He said they had arrived and were off to work. I don't expect to hear from them for another week. It's going to be hard work and long hours. I once did a summer fighting fires, and this situation sounds similar. They'll have to be on alert for the next few weeks, treating all kinds of injuries."

"But they're okay, right?" Amber asked, forgetting that she was trying not to talk.

"They are with professionals, Amber," Kathleen said. "And they are in an area where they may not have access to a phone. Are you worried?"

Amber nodded.

"Is that why you aren't sleeping?" Kathleen asked.

They waited as she finished chewing, and Amber finally spoke. "Yes."

"What are you most worried about?"

"You need to tell them, Amber. Or I will," Jade said from the doorway.

"Shut up, Jade!" Amber yelled.

"That's no way to talk to your sister!" Roy's booming voice startled all of them.

"What is it that you aren't saying?" Roy said, now that he had their attention. "Have you been reading past dark again?"

Amber whimpered, and Kathleen pulled her into her lap. The girl was obviously scared. Did Roy yell at them a lot? *How dare he?*

"She's been staying up and watching the news about the earthquake," Jade said. "And waiting for them to phone."

"Jade!" Amber cried. "I hate you!"

Kathleen held Amber close, rocking her. "Is that true?"

She glanced across at Roy, who was looking between the three, exasperated. The images on the news were disturbing for a child. Particularly one who knew her parents were there.

"Didn't you hear the television?" she asked Roy.

"No. Once I fall asleep, I don't hear much," he said, looking apologetic.

"Amber, I want you to stay away from the television at night from now on. If you have questions, you can ask your grandpa and me. We can look at the news together and talk about it. I know it's scary to have them so far away. But your parents are being a big help, and they will phone when they can."

Amber nodded, eyes cast down toward her plate.

"She's looking at the Facebook page too," said Jade.

"I hate you." Amber's eyes flashed at Jade, and if looks could kill, Amber would have been an only child by now.

"What are you doing on the computer without supervision?" asked Roy. "You know you aren't allowed on the computer without us."

"I needed to know what was happening."

"Well, Facebook isn't always accurate," said Kathleen in the calmest voice she could manage. She needed to de-escalate this. Roy was vibrating, and the last thing they needed was for him to explode.

"They show more than what's on the news," said Amber defensively.

"Yes, but there is no telling who is posting there, or what their sources are."

"What does that mean?" asked Jade, treading softly into the kitchen again and sitting on Roy's lap.

"It means that when you read about something, you need to think about who is sharing the information, how much they actually know about the situation, where they are getting their information from, and whether the story has had the facts checked or not. Not all the things you read on the Internet are accurate."

"Oh," said Amber. "So some of the pictures might not be real?"

"Or they could be a very small part of the big picture," said Kathleen. "Tell you what. Why don't we send your parents a text message so they know we are thinking of them? Then we can try to arrange a time for them to phone and talk to us all. Okay?" Kathleen wished she had thought of this before. Why hadn't she realized how worried the girls would be? All she had been thinking about what how to spend time with them. She hadn't been thinking about what they needed.

She hugged Amber a little closer and then reached for her cell phone to pull up an app and send a text to Nicole.

"Let's send your mother a note right now. She'll get it first thing in the morning."

"Okay. Can we tell them we got a Christmas tree?" Jade asked.

"Yes, of course. We can even take a picture of it when it's decorated and send it to them."

"But we'll have to get it decorated first. Who wants to help me put on the lights?" Roy asked.

"I do," said Jade.

"Well, why don't we make a batch of scones while they're doing that?" Kathleen said to Amber.

"Your Christmas Cranberry Scones?"

"Yes, the Christmas Cranberry Scones."

"That sounds good," said Roy. "It's a deal. Come on, Jade, let's get the lights on the tree, and then we can get Nana's treat."

He guided Jade out of the room, and then looked back at Kathleen and mouthed the words *thank you*.

She smiled, mouthed, *You're welcome*, and gave Amber one more hug before scooching her granddaughter off her lap and heading to the counter to unpack the baking supplies.

CHAPTER 10

The next day, Roy and Pat forewent the forest path, now muddy from rains, and opted instead to run on the treadmill at the gym and take a good long soak in the hot tub afterward.

It also gave Pat the opportunity to ask questions. "So Kathleen's been there every night?"

"Uh-huh," Roy murmured. Maybe if he was uncommunicative, Pat would give up and mind his own business so they could appreciate a good soak in peace.

"What's she like these days? Is she as intense as she was when we were young?"

"Intense?"

"You know. Always trying too hard. She had to always be the best at everything —student president, top student. Intense."

"She's still organized. I think that's where Nicole gets it from. She's a spreadsheet person."

"Is she organizing you, too?"

"No, not really. More like strongly suggesting I do things." Like the way she had insisted he make a doctor's appointment. The way Lois might have done. The way someone who cared about you did. He had missed that.

Pat laughed. "Yes, my ex-wife used to do that. I didn't listen, which is probably why she's my ex."

"Well, Kathleen isn't my wife, just my co-kidsitter, so it will be fine. At least we're getting along better than we used to."

"Maybe she's finally forgiving you," said Pat.

"For what?"

Pat just looked at him. "You're kidding, right?"

"No, I have no idea why she stopped talking to me. Or to Lois. Lois would never say. She said they grew apart and that I should just let it go." Which had been easy to do until his son fell in love with Kathleen's daughter, and Lois died, leaving him to face her alone. Now he had a distinct feeling others saw something he'd missed. Something important. But he didn't know what it was.

Pat was about to say something when two women from his building joined them in the hot tub. Pat introduced them, and Roy learned they were both widows. He would not get time to relax now. Widows made him uncomfortable. When Lois had first passed on, there had been one on his doorstep every day offering him dinner, or pie, or company, until he stopped answering the door and started spending time in his basement workshop, turning wood on his lathe to avoid them.

That first month he made a bowl a day, and then he moved on to chair legs and bases for lamps. It was honest work that got him away from people and reminded him who he was on his own.

The only people he had let into the workshop were Pat, Jason, and Jade, none of whom had relationship designs on him. And Lois, of course. He still had her ashes there in an urn on the shelf, where he could talk to her every day. That first month, he'd only used the rest of his house for eating and, finally, falling asleep on the couch in front of the television.

He listened to the conversation, and though the women seemed nice, he didn't want to stay. Anyway, he had an appointment, so he told Pat he had to go. Pat waved him off and turned his attention back to the women, one of whom seemed to have his interest.

Roy silently wished him good luck— anything to help him wriggle out of being a wingman in the future—and left to go to the doctor. He'd promised Kathleen.

I don't have time to do that," Roy said to the doctor an hour later. "Is it that important?"

"There are rarely openings this time of year, and, if you wait, it could take until well into January to get into the sleep lab," she said.

"But an entire night in Victoria? I have my granddaughters to watch."

"I think it's best, yes. You say you've been falling asleep often, needing naps, and that you nearly nodded off while driving the other day. I need to rule out sleep apnea before I do a barrage of other tests."

"And the blood tests?"

"Routine. To look at when I consider the sleep study results. It's important, Roy. What will you do if the kids are in the car, and you fall asleep?"

She made a good point. "Okay, so tomorrow? What time do I have to be there?"

"It's an overnight thing. You can show up at seven to the hospital. They'll get you settled in, hook you up so they can monitor your heart rate and your breathing, and then you go to sleep, and they monitor you for the night. Best to leave early and take time to rest halfway there, though, if you are in danger of nodding off. Better yet, is there someone who could take you?"

"I'll see if I can get a friend to drive me," he said, considering whether Pat might like a reason to go to the city. First, he had to ask Kathleen to stay at the house tomorrow night and get the girls off to school. He would be back by the end of the day to pick them up. "But either way, I'll be there." He might as well get it over with.

He thanked her and left the clinic, picking up a brochure on sleep apnea on the way out. If he had this condition, he wanted to know what he was up against.

On his way back to the house, he stopped by Kathleen's store to see her in person. She may need time to arrange help, and he wanted to reassure her he would be back as early as he could the morning after the test.

When he pushed open the door, a little bell tinkled, a sound he liked much better than the buzzing some stores had these days. There were a few customers browsing, and one of Kathleen's staff was helping a woman at the counter. Kathleen wasn't to be seen.

While he waited for the cashier to finish with her customer, he looked around. The tree looked great, and the train set was a nice touch. The kids could come in and push a button, making the train travel around its route before it stopped in front of the window again. *Clever.* She had done a lot to improve the atmosphere, too. It was bright but cozy, and she had a range of toys to choose from. He could see why she enjoyed selling toys. It would be a fun place to spend your days.

The customer at the cash register took her bag and left the store, so he stepped up to the cash, introduced himself, and asked where he could find Kathleen.

"Oh, she's in the back." The woman pointed, then turned her attention to another customer loaded down with toys.

Sidestepping several kids, he made his way to the door. It was slightly ajar. Peering inside, he found Kathleen there, instructing a young man to be careful with a bulky package he was passing to her. They were unpacking merchandise from a stack of boxes. He stood quietly for a minute, watching her work. She looked tired, or maybe stressed? He hoped she would have time to stay with the kids. It was a lot to ask, but the doctor had been adamant that he do this sooner than later.

"Josh, we've gone through them all. We'll have to make a list now of what we have, and then I'll try some other suppliers to see what we can get in." She sounded agitated. This was not going to go well.

She turned toward the door of her little office and stopped when she saw him standing there. "Roy, what are you doing here? Are the kids okay?"

"The kids are fine. I just came to ask you a huge favor." He braced himself for her reaction. The Kathleen he knew had a habit of losing it when she was stressed.

"Sure, just a second." She waited for Josh to unload a box of puzzles and electronic games, then held the door open for him as he wheeled the load out to the floor of the store.

"What's up?" she asked, turning to Roy.

"I went to the doctor, and she wants to send me to do a test in Victoria tomorrow."

"What time"—she looked at him warily—"do you need me to drive you?"

"No, it's not that. It's a test where I have to stay overnight at the hospital and then come back the next morning. I can drive myself. I just need someone—I need you—to stay overnight at the house and watch the kids. I'll have to leave early afternoon, so I won't be able to pick them up after school, either. I know it's a lot to ask this time of year..."

"Of course," she said. "I'll just have to rearrange the schedule a bit. Not to worry." That was easier than he thought it would be. What was she up to?

"Great, I'll see you tonight and we can discuss the details."

She was looking at him strangely, like she wanted to ask him something and then thought better of it. He waited a few more seconds, trying to think of something else to say, reluctant to leave.

"Was there something else?" she asked, and he realized he had just been standing there, staring.

He shook his head. "No, no. Listen, you're busy. I'll let you get back to work."

"Yes, of course. I'll see you tonight."

She stood aside as he turned to leave. Her hair was slightly ruffled, the way it used to be when they were kids, climbing trees. He had a sudden urge to ruffle it some more, as he would've back then, and tell her everything would be okay. Instead, he turned and left. He had no business thinking about Kathleen as anything but what she was: his son's bossy mother-in-law and the woman who had betrayed his wife and broken her heart.

He called Pat when he got back to the house and was relieved when Pat agreed to accompany him to the city. "I can stay with my son for the night," Pat said. "And it gives me a chance to see my grandson."

"Thanks, Pat."

"What time do you want to leave? If we go early enough, we can get some shopping in. I have a couple of gifts to buy."

Gifts. He had completely forgotten about gifts.

"We can leave right after I drop the girls at school."

He was hopeless at buying gifts. Lois was the one who'd bought gifts. And since Lois had died, Nicole had helped him.

Having Pat along would be great. He was good at that sort of thing. Roy thought about Kathleen's store and the stacks of gifts on her shelves. Maybe he should spend his money in her store, and get her help with selecting—

Abruptly he shook his head. *No.* No, he had asked enough of Kathleen.

CHAPTER 11

The next afternoon, Kathleen slammed down her office phone after pleading for nearly twenty minutes with her most prominent toy distributor. Clenching her fists, she screamed, hearing too late the knock on her door.

She rose from her seat and pulled the door open to find Josh there, just in time for his afternoon shift.

He drew back his tall lanky frame, looking younger in his uncertainty. Normally he was confident, brazen even, but now he looked like he might be afraid.

She quickly smiled. "It's fine, Josh. I just have a problem with one of our distributers. I've been trying to get a rush delivery, but they can't accommodate me."

"You mean for the Christmas crafts? What are you going to do? We're so close to Christmas."

"Well, today I'm going to pick up my granddaughters and take them home and make them dinner. What you can do while it is quiet, and while Jackie is still here to look after customers, is finish the work we started yesterday. Go through the inventory of items we have the most stock in." She beckoned him into the office and pulled up the information on the computer to show him where she entered and tracked the inventory. "Once you have double-checked the numbers, send me a list in an email."

"You trust me to do this?"

She paused a moment to look him straight in the eye. "You want to be an entrepreneur, right?"

"Yes." He nodded.

"Then I think it's time you learned more about business, particularly how to solve the problems that can arise at the last minute."

"I won't let you down, Kathleen." The young man was looking at her in earnest.

"I know you won't," Kathleen said, turning away from the computer to look at him. "I trust you."

He smiled tentatively, straightening up to his full height.

"And Josh," she added, "if you or Casey have any ideas about promoting some of those items you find, send those too. I need to revamp this week's newsletter."

"I can do that." He was grinning now; the old confident Josh was back.

"Thanks, Josh." She left the store and headed to get the girls. They would help get her mind off things. She found that distracting her brain for a while often gave it time to come up with answers to her looming questions. Hopefully that would happen today, because she had a lot of questions.

"Can we do some more baking?" Amber asked when she picked them up from school.

"Yeah, Nana! I never got to help last time," said Jade.

"Well, you know, that's not such a bad idea," she said. "We could even bake the walls of a gingerbread house and put it all together tomorrow night if you'd like."

"A real gingerbread house?"

"We never made one of those before."

"Well, we can do one today, then. We will need to design it and bake it. Then tomorrow I can get some decorations on the way home from work, and we can put it all together."

They made three different kinds of cookies. First the gingerbread, then chocolate chip, and finally a batch of candy cane cookies from a recipe she'd had since she was a child.

"These are just like the ones Grandma used to make," said Amber as they were rolling the red-tinted dough and the white dough into strips and twisting them together so they looked like candy canes.

"Your Grandma Lois and I used to make them together," she said. "Her mother showed us how."

"You used to be friends with Grandma?" asked Jade, her little face doubtful.

"Yes, we lived just down the street from each other. That's how your mom and dad met."

"What do you mean?"

"Well, my mother—your mom's grandmother—lived next door to your dad's grandmother. So, when your mom and dad were little, they would see each other most summers when your mom visited your great-grandmother."

"I didn't know that," said Jade, reaching for some more dough to roll. "These are going to be nice, aren't they, Nana?" She put the next cane onto the cookie sheet.

"I think they are turning out just fine," said Kathleen.

"Why weren't you friends with Grandma afterward?" Amber asked.

"Well, I guess we just lost touch," Kathleen said, taking out a piece of paper to make a pattern for the gingerbread house. It had been a while, but she was sure she could still do it.

"Dad said you didn't really get along with Grandma."

"I see. Your dad told you that?"

"He said it to Mom, and she said she didn't know why either. They were worried about leaving you with us," said Amber apologetically.

"But we think you are getting along just fine. Don't we, Amber?" Jade reached over to pat her on the arm.

"So why didn't you and Grandma get along?"

Kathleen looked from one to the other, deciding to tell them what they could understand. The truth. Maybe she just needed to tell someone the truth, even though Lois had certainly known. She had even apologized the last time they'd spoken, saying she regretted her actions.

"Well. When we were very young, I told your grandmother that I liked a boy, and then it turned out that she liked him too. I was hurt when the boy decided to go out with her instead, I guess."

The bare-bones facts didn't tell the real tale, of course. Not the part where Kathleen had confided in Lois that she had loved Roy since they were little and wanted to marry him when they grew up. Not the part where Lois had laughed at her, looked her up and down, stared at her flat chest, thin limbs, and freckles, and said, "A boy like Roy wouldn't want a little girl like you."

And not the part where she had woken at the camping trip she, Lois, Roy, and

Patrick had taken after graduation, only to find Lois missing.

She had climbed out of the tent into the quiet morning air. It was crisp, and dew had settled on the grass. She pulled on her boots and walked to Roy's tent to see if he and Pat were still asleep. Peeking in, she found them: Lois entwined in Roy's arms, a satisfied smile on her lips.

Kathleen had been grabbed from behind then, a hand over her mouth, and found herself being dragged away by Patrick. "Come on, Kat," he'd said. "I'm sorry. I didn't want you to find out this way."

She had sobbed on Patrick's shoulder for a long time, and he held her close.

"What does he see in her?" she asked over and over.

"I don't know, Kat. I don't know."

They finally heard voices from the pair as they emerged from the tent.

"Pat?" yelled Roy.

Pat looked at her and silently asked if she was ready to face them.

"We're here," he called out.

Footsteps got closer, and tears threatened to spout again. Pat just kept his arm around her. "Shh. It'll be okay. You and I are destined for more, Kat. Remember that."

And she had tried to remember that when she saw Lois's self-satisfied smile, her proprietary arm on Roy's, and the way Roy looked down at Lois as though she were the only person there. It was the final straw. Their friendship, if it had ever been a friendship, was over. Kathleen was done.

They packed to leave that day, and she rarely spoke to Lois or Roy afterward. When she was invited back for the wedding that September to be a third bridesmaid—the maid of honor and other two slots were held by Lois's cousins—she had been glad of the excuse that she was in the middle of her first semester and had assignments due. And, when Jason was born nine months later, she hadn't returned for the shower.

"Well, Nana," Jade said, bringing her back to the conversation, "that just proves that boys are dumb. They like to ruin everything. I wouldn't let a dumb boy get between me and my friends."

"Boys aren't dumb," said Amber. "Dad's not dumb, and Grandpa's not dumb."

Jade considered this point for a moment. "Well, little boys are kind of dumb. Like Zac Kimble. I don't like Zac Kimble."

"Zac's okay," said Amber. "You just don't like that he's better at basketball."

"You take that back," said Jade. "He's not better."

"Okay, okay," said Amber, backing away from her sister and laughing. "But he's pretty good."

"That's true," said Jade, rolling out some more dough. "But I'm still better."

Kathleen listened to their chatter, grateful that their laser-focused curiosity had deviated from her to other subjects. She finished cutting out the pattern and rolled out more gingerbread dough as they continued to talk. Then she showed the girls how to lay the pattern on the dough and cut out the walls and roof and doors.

When they were done, and the gingerbread walls were laid out on cookie sheets, she said, "Okay, you two, off to bed with you now. I'll bake the rest of these cookies tonight, and tomorrow night we can decorate them and make the rum balls."

When the girls were in bed, and she was cleaning up in the kitchen, she turned her mind to the problems of the day and to their conversation.

She still had no idea what she could use to decorate the tree at the store. Perhaps there were some gingerbread kits she could get in at the last minute. Building one for the bottom of the tree might be a nice touch. She'd noticed them at the bakery next door. If they hadn't entered the festival with their own tree, maybe they would agree to collaborate.

The phone rang as she was settling into the big comfy couch to watch a little television. "Hello?"

"Hi." Roy's comforting, deep voice spoke to her from the other end of the line. "I just wanted to make sure everything was going okay."

"We're okay. We made cookies and the walls for a gingerbread house. They've both just gone to bed, but I'll tell them you called when they wake up tomorrow."

"And how are you? Did you get your order figured out yesterday after I left? You seemed concerned about that."

Mmm, he had noticed—and taken the time to ask.

"I'll have to come up with another solution to my Christmas tree entry for the festival next weekend," she said. "I was going to use the contents of a Christmas craft kit to make the ornaments, and then have a picture of the box under the tree. Well, that's not happening. I'll have to come up with another idea—something that kids can make with their families. Something interactive. Meanwhile, I thought a gingerbread house and gingerbread people could be part of the display. There are kits out there for that. I don't know. I'm sure something will come to mind. I just need to have some of it in stock in case it strikes an interest in people.

"Well, I'm sure you'll think of something."

"What time will you be back tomorrow?"

"Pat's here, and he wants to pick up a few more gifts in the morning. But we'll be home by three, in time to get the girls from school."

"I'll see you for dinner, then. I've left some salmon out to defrost." *Gifts.* Well, at least she had been proactive about that this year. She almost always had her shopping done by early September. But she didn't have anything for Roy. She would have to think of something.

"That sounds good. I have a recipe for salmon fillets you might like," he said. "I'll cook."

"I would like that," she said, starting to imagine all the other things she would like Roy to do for her... with her. To her. She put her hand to her mouth at the unbidden thoughts—what memories had that conversation with the kids dredged up in her mind? She had to stop this train of thought before it derailed into a large messy pile of baggage she didn't want to unpack. She had to go. This was nice, but Roy wasn't for her. He still wore his wedding ring, for heaven's sake. "I have to turn in now," she said. "I need to get an early start, so I'll see you tomorrow night, okay?"

"I'm looking forward to it," he said, a smile in his warm voice. "Good night, Kat."

She clicked off the phone and flung it to the other side of the couch. How dare he call her Kat? She was no longer that young naive girl who had climbed trees with him. Their friendship had ended long ago.

It had been years since she first realized she couldn't count on a man. They would eventually leave you for someone else, or betray your trust, or both. Her father had left to start a new family, abandoning her, her mother, and her little brothers. Then her own husband left to start a new family with Jolene. And Roy had chosen Lois over her, even though they were friends long before Lois moved to town. She cringed, thinking how childish she sounded. But no matter. It had been a part of her education—that she could only ever really rely on herself.

Jade was right. Boys were dumb.

CHAPTER 12

Roy and Pat spent the next morning wandering around the mall, trying to find just the right baseball glove for Pat's grandson.

"What are you going to get for Kathleen?" Pat asked as they walked past a jewelry store.

"I hadn't thought of that," he said. "We're just barely civil again."

"Well, don't you think she'll be expecting something?"

"I don't see why."

"Well, if Jason and Nicole get back after Christmas, you are going to have to do it alone, and you know the girls will be watching to see if you exchange gifts."

Why did Pat always have to make a good point? The girls *would* be watching, and what if she got him something and he didn't reciprocate? Disaster.

"What would you suggest?" he asked. For a man who had been divorced for so long, Pat seemed to really understand what women liked.

"Something from the heart," Pat said. "I'm going to see if I can find the right size ball glove." He pointed to a sports store. "I should have got it when they were in season. Why don't you see what you can find? I'll meet you out at the door we came in"—he glanced at his watch—"in, say, an hour?"

"Sure," Roy said, walking away with no intention of producing a present that Pat could mock in the next hour. Instead, he stopped in front of a toy store. Maybe he would find something for the girls there.

He walked inside and realized it sold nothing but interlocking blocks. The displays were intriguing. One was a castle with a dragon on the roof and a moat below. Another was a Santa village, and a third display was a horse ranch complete with horses. Just like the horses in Amber's books.

When he finally left the store, he had two kits: the castle and the horse ranch, and a small box of pieces. He could introduce them to the girls that evening so he could get them interested in using them. That took care of the girls.

When the hour was up, he met Pat and had to admit that he hadn't found anything for Kathleen.

"What does she like?" asked Pat.

"We haven't really spent much time talking except for swapping some old stories and talking about the kids."

"Well, maybe you should get to know her a bit better. She's available. You know about most of her baggage. And it's not like you're interested in meeting new women. You got out of that hot tub so fast the other day it was like you'd been bitten by a shark or something."

"I had an appointment."

"You didn't even try to engage, Roy. They are nice women. In fact, I think I'm going to ask Bridget out for dinner when I get back. She's fun, and I need a bit more fun in my life."

"I've got enough people in my life," mumbled Roy.

"Exactly," said Pat, "and one of those people is Kathleen. You really should take a closer look at her. She's pretty special, and you two have been friends since you were six."

"Correction: we *were* friends. Now we are just in-laws. I'm not ready for a relationship, Pat. Besides, Kathleen isn't interested in me. She's been avoiding me for years."

"You're hopeless," said Pat. "And of course she's not going to try very hard.

You're still wearing your wedding ring. You're still talking to Lois every night. You haven't moved on. No woman would want to put up with that."

"Pat, let's change the subject before we say things we shouldn't. It's a long drive."

"Suits me," said Pat, pulling on to the highway and turning up the music on the radio. "It's your life."

~

That evening, Roy seared the salmon and added some herbs he'd picked up on his way to get the girls from school. The house smelled of fresh tarragon, basil, and lemon.

"Mmm, that smells so good," Kathleen said when she entered the kitchen just in time for dinner, carrying a grocery sack.

She unloaded the contents onto the counter. Gumdrops, icing sugar, food coloring, sprinkles—a plethora of items they could use to decorate the house and cookies.

"You have enough candy to decorate a real house there," he laughed.

"One can never have too much candy this time of year," she said. "Can I help you with anything?"

"No, I've got it. Just let the girls know that it's time for dinner."

They ate another enjoyable meal around the table. The girls told them about their day, and Kathleen shared a text from their parents, who said they were working hard but missing the girls.

"They are okay, then," Amber said.

"Of course," said Jade. "They are with professionals—right, Nana?"

Kathleen glanced at Roy and smiled, sharing a look between adults over a child's remarks. Jade was reflecting exactly what they had told her only a few days earlier.

"That's right," said Kathleen. "And your parents know what they're doing."

"And we need to make the house perfect for when they come back," said Amber.

"Including a real gingerbread house!" Jade said.

"You two finish up, clear away the dishes, and I'll get the mixer out to make the royal icing. It is a stiff icing that we can use to put the house together. Then you can help me decorate it, and the gingerbread people."

Roy leaned back to watch the girls clear the plates and wash up. Kathleen had them working together like a well-oiled machine, the way she always did. She was just like the friend he remembered from their younger days. Except she wasn't that young girl anymore.

She asked him if he wanted to help, and he declined. "Call me when it's time to make the rum balls, though. I can help with that.

CHAPTER 13

Kathleen and the girls worked for the next couple of hours on their projects, and she was delighted with the final product. The house looked sturdy—a good thing in a gingerbread house—and the roof looked as though it were really thatched.

The girls stood back and admired their work.

"What do you think?" she asked.

"I think we should send a picture to Mom and Dad," said Amber.

"Yeah! They'll never believe we made this all by ourselves."

"I'm gonna get Grandpa to come see," said Jade. "And tell him it's time to make rum balls!"

"Rum balls? Did I hear someone say rum balls?" Roy came into the kitchen just then and stopped in his tracks, shock on his face. "Did you make that all by yourselves?" he asked the girls, his eyes twinkling as he looked up at Kathleen.

"Yes, yes," said Jade and Amber together. "We did."

"Nana helped," said Amber, glancing over at Kathleen.

"But they did the roof and the path and the trees…"

"Look, Grandpa—see how we put the candy together to make the trees?"

"And now we are going to make rum balls. You can help if you want," Jade said. "But you have to wash your hands first."

"I'll be back in a few minutes," said Kathleen. Then we can get started."

She went down the hall to use the bathroom, and when she returned, she could hear them all talking.

"What else did you do while I was away?" he was asking. She slowed and listened. It would be nice to know what they liked best about the day before. It would help her figure out what else they could do over the next couple of weeks.

"We made sugar cookies."

"And I played basketball."

"And Nana told us why she didn't like Grandma Lois," said Amber.

Kathleen sighed. It was never a good idea to eavesdrop. You pretty much never heard a good thing about yourself. She lifted her hand to push open the kitchen door.

"Really?" he asked.

"They both liked the same boy," said Jade. "Even though Nana Kathleen liked him first."

"Hmm," she heard Roy say. Kathleen wondered if she had better interrupt them now or wait for a few minutes. Maybe she should just leave? This was humiliating.

"And did she tell you his name?"

"No," said Amber. "It was a long, long time ago. Besides, he ended up marrying someone else."

"And Nana ended up marrying Grandpa Chris."

"And it was all just in the past. But after she went to school, it was too hard to come back and make friends again."

"Did Nana say that?"

"No, but that's what happened with me and Jenny Lee when we stopped being friends last year," said Jade. "She got new friends, and I got new friends, and so she isn't my best friend anymore."

"So who's ready to make rum balls?" Kathleen asked, finally gathering the courage to step into the room. "I'll get the butter."

Roy and the girls looked guilty, caught in the act of discussing her behind her back, but she pretended she hadn't heard.

"Amber, you get me the rolled oats. Jade, you can bring the cocoa and the icing sugar."

She set up the mixer and measured the butter into the bowl to cream it, ignoring the way he was looking at her. He seemed angry. Well, if he wanted to be angry that she had been in love with him, then so be it. It wasn't like she could do anything about the past.

He watched her now through narrowed eyes as she and the girls measured and added the ingredients.

"What did you do today, Nana?" Jade asked. "Did you finish decorating the Christmas tree?

"The staff did that on Sunday," Kathleen said, still aware that she was being watched by a silent Roy. "I've been trying to solve a conundrum."

"A conn-what?" asked Jade.

"A conundrum, a problem. I've been trying to figure out what to use as decorations on my tree for the festival. The decorations I ordered haven't arrived, and so I need to figure out something else. And before next Tuesday. That's the deadline for the trees to be set up in the hall."

"What about candy canes?"

"Or paper snowflakes? We make those at school."

"Or, I know—you could make gingerbread people! We can even help you!!"

"All really good ideas," Kathleen said. "We are just about done here. We just need the rum. Roy? Could you reach it for me, please?"

He stopped glowering at her and walked to the cupboard where the liquor was kept, grabbing a bottle and handing it to her. What on earth was wrong with the man? He looked like he might bite.

"Thank you," she said, taking the bottle and measuring a tablespoon of rum into the mixture. "Here you go." She handed it back to him and he took it, but rather than putting it back up in the cupboard, he carried it into the living room.

"Is he mad?" Amber asked.

Jade shrugged.

"He's probably just tired," Kathleen said. "Let's get these rum balls rolled and put them into the freezer. And then," she said, "we can play a quick game of Yahtzee before I go."

"Can we have a sugar cookie and milk too?"

"That sounds like a great idea." Kathleen tried to keep her voice light, while her heart was breaking a little. She had let herself believe that maybe, just maybe, Roy was interested in at least being friends again. But apparently not. Learning that she had cared about him probably brought up memories of Lois.

Lois was always going to be between them, and she would never win him back. She had learned her lesson. Again.

Men were not meant to be part of her life. She was destined to be alone, and she decided she was good with that. At least she didn't have to risk being rejected because she loved someone. It was better to just avoid Roy in the future as much as possible.

CHAPTER 14

After Kathleen had safely tucked the girls into bed, she had come by the living room to let him know she was leaving.

He could have done more than grunt at the woman, but he didn't feel like being kind, or courteous, or even civil. She had lied to him, they all had, and he had never even known.

Pictures of the earthquake flickered on the television news in the darkness, but after a quarter bottle of rum, a drink he hadn't had in years, Roy barely registered what was being said. He did know that they were miraculously finding the occasional survivor in the rubble even now, over a week after the earthquake. That meant Jason and Nicole would be away at least another week, probably two, and that he would have to continue to play nice with Kathleen.

Why had Lois never told her that she and Kathleen had both been interested in the same boy at school? They had been married for decades. She had even taken her secret to the grave with her.

He went over and over their shared history in his mind and could come to only one conclusion. It must have been Patrick.

Pat had always been a ladies' man, and Lois and Kathleen had spent a lot of time with him. In fact, wasn't it Pat in whom Lois had confided when she was dying? Why had she gone to Pat rather than a girlfriend? Or tell him herself if she wanted him to move on after she died?

He knew why. It was because there was more to their relationship than Roy knew. Though Roy had done the right thing by Lois when she fell pregnant after they went camping together, it was Patrick she had always loved.

But why would that bother Kathleen? Unless she too also loved Patrick. Or maybe she knew about Lois and Patrick and was angry at the lie. Kathleen had never approved of people lying.

He needed to confront Pat about this. Or did he need to confront Kathleen? She had been his friend, and she had let him marry Lois without saying a damned thing. Maybe Jason wasn't even his. Was that why Pat was always visiting them, tossing the ball around with Jason when Roy was at work?

It certainly seemed that way. Though Jason did look a lot like Roy's own father, he and Pat had sported the same dark hair when they were growing up. The same brown eyes. In fact, people often asked if he and Pat were brothers, though they always assumed Pat was younger.

He was sure he was going to be sick, but first he needed to close his eyes.

A few hours later, he was jolted awake by the sound of knocking on the door. What time was it? He dragged up his wrist so he could see his watch. Seven in the morning? Who would be here that early?

There was another knock, and then he heard the key in the door. Kathleen. What was she doing here?

He had just struggled to his feet when she walked into the room.

"What are you doing here?" he asked.

"What do you think I'm doing here?" She had her hands on her hips, squared off like she was going to scream at him. He didn't need this first thing in the morning.

"Keep your voice down. The girls are still sleeping. Why are you here?"

"To make sure the girls get off to school okay. When I left, you were sitting there"—she pointed to the couch—"where you've obviously been all night, drinking and in a foul mood. What is wrong with you?"

"It isn't every day you find out your former best friend and your wife were in love with the same man your whole marriage. Were you ever going to tell me?"

"What are you talking about?"

"The girls told me last night that you and Lois had a falling out because you were both in love with the same boy in high school."

"So? Why would that make you so mad?"

"Because my whole marriage was a lie," he said. "I never knew."

"Would it have made a difference?"

"Of course it would have made a difference," he said. "I never would have married her if I'd known Jason wasn't mine."

They heard a toilet flush upstairs.

Kathleen lowered her voice to a fierce whisper. "What are you talking about? He was yours, all right. Lois made sure of that."

There were voices coming from the hallway now, and she backed up and away from him.

"Go upstairs and get cleaned up before they see you like this. Goodness, Roy! You look horrible."

He scowled at her. But she was right—the girls didn't need to see him with a hangover this morning.

"I'll take them to school," she said. "Just make sure you're presentable before they come home, okay?"

He left, chastened, and she walked into the living room to pick up the bottle of rum and empty glass he'd been using.

There were only two more weeks to get through. Maybe if he kept to his room when she was here it would be easier, but he had to be civil in front of the children. He had promised Nicole, and though Jason might not be his biological child, he was still his son. He had made a promise, and he intended to keep it.

CHAPTER 15

Kathleen left the store just before six and ran up to the house to make sure the girls were okay. Roy had been in a foul mood after finding out that she had been in love with him all through high school, and he hadn't been talking sense that morning.

What would make him think that Jason wasn't his child? Lois had been purposeful about not using protection that night. She thought back to the conversation that had ended their friendship so long ago.

"Of course I didn't use protection. How else do you think I would have got him?"

"You mean you got pregnant on purpose? Why would you do that?"

"Because I wanted him. I needed him."

"So you trapped him?"

"I just made sure it would be harder for him to leave," said Lois. "His parents were the ones who made him do the right thing."

"But you knew I loved him."

"I loved him more," Lois said, holding her hand over her stomach. "And I needed him more. At least you still have a father."

"Roy's not a replacement for your father," said Kathleen.

"No, he's going to be my husband," said Lois. "Remember that whenever you're in town. He's mine."

That was the last time Kathleen had spoken to her. After that, Kathleen made sure she left before the wedding to go to school. Made sure Lois wouldn't be around on the rare occasions when she visited. It had all gone well until twenty-five years later, when their children decided to marry.

When she got to the house, she saw the lights on in the kitchen. Hopefully that meant Roy was in better shape now. She used her key to go in and walked into the kitchen to find them all sitting around the table eating macaroni and cheese, something she rarely ate. She wasn't hungry anyway.

"Hi, Nana, do you want some dinner?"

"No, thank you. I ate a late lunch," she said. "I just stopped by to see if you guys were okay. I need to go home and do some work."

"We're fine," said Roy.

"Grandpa bought us some of those interlocking blocks as a treat," said Jade.

"Yeah," said Amber. "We're going to build a house."

"Like a gingerbread house but made of blocks," said Jade.

"Well, I can't wait to see it. Maybe tomorrow when I get back you can show it to me."

"Okay!"

"It's my turn to put away the dishes," said Roy. "You two go set up the blocks on the coffee table. I'll be there soon."

When the girls had left the room, she turned to him. "It looks like you have everything under control."

"Yes. I think we're good for the next few days. You don't have to come every night. I've got a routine now. I'll be fine."

Kathleen's heart began to pound faster. Why was he doing this? If he didn't care about her, it was fine, but to keep her away from the children? That was just wrong. "What about the sailpast?"

He frowned and looked at the door to the living room. "You can pick them up that evening and take them for a few hours. It will give me some time to work in the shop."

"Are you still bringing them to the festival next weekend?"

"Yes. We'll be there," he said. "Thanks, Kathleen, for all your help. I'll call if I need anything. I'm sure you will welcome the break so you can get some work done."

"What exactly have I done to offend you?" she asked.

"Nothing. Everything is fine. I simply think that we have asked too much of you the past week or so."

"They are my grandchildren too, you know. I enjoy looking after them."

His eyes shifted downward. Good. At least he looked a little ashamed of himself.

"Kathleen, I have been trying to deal with Lois's death for two years, and being around you just reminds me of how much I've lost. I'm sorry. I just need some space. Maybe you can have the girls Saturday night? They could do a sleepover at your house. Would that work?"

"That will be fine," she said, trying to keep the tears back. She was not going to cry in front of him. She was going to be the bigger person for Nicole and for the girls. Whatever was going on with Roy was his problem. Not hers.

"But what about your tendency to fall asleep? Have you worked that out yet?"

He was glaring at her now. "Not that it's any of your concern, but I have been diagnosed with sleep apnea. I'm getting a CPAP machine later today, so I will be just fine."

"Good," she said, leaving the room before she said anything more. At least he wouldn't be dropping off to sleep. That made her rest easier.

She stopped by the living room to let the girls know that she wouldn't be coming for the next few days. "But I'll see you on Saturday. And on Sunday, maybe you can help me make tree ornaments for the Christmas festival tree."

"What kind of ornaments, Nana?"

"I'm not sure yet. But I'll let you know." She drove downtown to the store. That was one thing she still needed to do: call a staff meeting and get some ideas from Josh and Casey. And then she would figure out what to do, even if it took her all night.

CHAPTER 16

On Friday, after dropping the girls at school, Roy sat in the living room, listening to "Blue Christmas" over and over. It was the song Lois had always played this time of year in memory of her father, and now he played it in memory of her because on this date, two years before, she had died.

At ten in the morning, there was loud knocking on the door, and he went to answer it. "What do you want now?" he asked as he opened the door. But it wasn't Kathleen. It was Pat.

"Where the hell have you been?" Pat asked, stepping over the threshold and barging into the house. "I've been calling you for three days, and you haven't answered the phone."

"I'm sitting here with Elvis."

"Have you been doing this for three days?"

"No. Of course not."

"Why didn't you answer my calls? We went through this week together last year. Why are you pushing me away?"

"Because you aren't welcome. I don't want to be reminded that she loved you and married me."

"What are you talking about?"

"Your affair with my wife. How long did it go on?"

"I never had an affair with your wife!"

"So it was just before we were married?"

"Roy, read my lips: I never had an affair with Lois. Ever."

"But you knew she loved you."

"Roy, Lois was head over heels for you. She only tolerated me because I was your friend."

"No, you're wrong."

"What makes you think I'm lying? How long have we known each other?"

"The girls said that Kathleen and Lois were in love with the same man. That's why Kat left. It had to be you. Who else would it have been?"

Patrick looked at the ceiling and shook his head. "You idiot. Roy, Kathleen and Lois were both in love with you. That's why Kat left. And she didn't speak to Lois because she thought you had been trapped into marriage."

Roy sat down on the couch, feeling as though he had been kicked.

"That can't be right. Kat and I were friends. She didn't love me." But as he said it, he remembered the kiss they'd shared. The way Kat had always been there for him. And he realized it was true.

He pulled his hand over his face and looked up at Pat. "What have I done?"

"I don't know what you've done. We haven't spoken in days."

"We were getting along so well. Like we were before Lois and I got together. Before that, Kat had always been there, from the time we were in grade one. After she left town, it was like a big piece of me left with her. But by then, Jason was on the way. Then I was married. I had to work hard at the bank and do all those night-school courses so I could get a better paying job... There was no time. I thought it was because of the work, because of having to be an adult. I had no idea..."

"Roy, you've lost me."

"It was always Kat. Kat and Lois were a dynamic duo, but it was always Kat who was there for both of us. When I chose Lois, she must have felt so betrayed."

"Yeah. I know."

"Why didn't you tell me?"

"When would I have done that? I was at school, remember? Kat and I left town at the same time. It wasn't until I came home that we could have talked about it, and by then you had a three-month-old, a home, a family. What would have been the point?"

"I just wish I'd known."

"You were happy with Lois. You two made it. Kat moved on. There was nothing more we could do."

"I told her to leave. I told her I didn't want her to come by every night. I basically rejected her again."

"Well, maybe it's for the best. Why let her fall for you again only to rip the rug out from under her? It's obvious you haven't moved on. No one wants a third person in their relationship. Even if they are dead."

"I'm moving on."

"Yeah, then what's with the 'Blue Christmas'? And the wedding band? You haven't moved on, Roy. Maybe you never will. And unless you do, she's better off without you. Kat is too nice a woman to get hurt again."

CHAPTER 17

The bell over the store door tinkled for the hundredth time that morning, and Kathleen forced herself to stay on task. Even the delighted look of the customers as they rediscovered the store wasn't enough to jog her out of the mood she was in.

After putting in a rush order with several suppliers, she still only had stock in a few items. What was she supposed to do now?

She scanned the items on the list of stock she had in store, wracking her brain for an idea. She had several extra superheroes and a few extra dolls and puzzles, but what she seemed to have most were sets of interlocking plastic building blocks that could be used to construct houses and even villages.

She looked at the stuffed toys list. Some were small enough to place on the tree, but a teddy bear theme wasn't nearly as interesting as handmade glass balls filled with glitter and colored paints.

The staff had suggested some good ideas when she brought them together, and she had been able to get the bakery next door to collaborate with her—the gingerbread people could hang on the tree, and the two houses could sit at the bottom, bearing the names of their stores—but then what? She needed a solution. Fast.

She only had three more days to get it all figured out, and with the sailpast it would be a busy weekend. Shoppers had been streaming into the store the whole week, and she had spent the last three days working nonstop, changing the marketing plans to incorporate last-minute shipments of toys. At least some of the higher-end robots and educational toys were available. They meant more revenue. All she had to do was sell them and the surplus of blocks in the back room. Maybe she could get the girls to build her a store out of blocks for the bottom of the tree. She would ask them the next morning when she picked them up.

She hoped Roy had been doing okay this week. In spite of what he had said, Nicole had reminded her that today was the anniversary of Lois's death, and that he'd had a hard time getting through it the year before.

She was glad she had called Pat to let him know Roy might need him. Pat said he'd drop by, so she was sure he would. He was a good friend.

The little bell over the front door tinkled again, reminding her that it was time to relieve people for their breaks. She didn't have time to dwell on Roy and Pat.

She had to think of a theme to go with the gingerbread house. Withdrawing her entry into the festival wasn't an option.

CHAPTER 18

Roy climbed out of the shower, shaved, and dressed in warm clothes. He wanted to be ready to face Kathleen, and if it meant attending the sailpast at her condo—and on her turf—so be it. It wasn't like she could refuse him. The kids would be watching, and she *had* invited him, albeit before he had banned her from the house. But an invitation was an invitation.

When she arrived at four to get the girls, he was ready for her. He even had a gift, one he knew she needed desperately. He had sworn the girls to secrecy.

"Hello, Kathleen," he said, joining them in the hallway where the girls were waiting.

"Roy." She had a tinge of ice in her voice.

Hmm. He had always enjoyed a challenge.

"Wondering if I could join you tonight after all."

"Yeah!" said Jade.

"That would be great, wouldn't it, Nana?" said Amber.

She looked from one to the other and then scowled at him. "Of course. I've got enough dinner for all of us."

"How about I drive?" said Roy. "I don't think I'll fit in your little car."

She looked up at him and then outside at the Mini. "No, I don't suppose you will. But how will I get my car later?"

"Don't worry, I'll drive you where you need to go."

She looked at him and then at the anxious faces of the girls before nodding and pasting a smile on her face. She wasn't happy, but hopefully when she saw what he and the girls had in the back of the truck, she would be pleased.

He helped the girls and Kathleen climb into the truck, and they headed downtown.

"How's business?" he said as he drove, trying to get her to smile or at least speak to him.

"We've been busy," she said.

"Have you found your theme for the tree yet?"

He heard giggles from the back seat and looked into the rearview mirror to warn the pair to be quiet.

"I have half of it planned," she said. "The bakery has agreed to enter a collaboration tree this year."

"That sounds tasty," he said, as though he hadn't already heard about her plans from Josh the week before. He had learned a lot from Josh during that discussion, while Kathleen had been busy in the back. Nice young man.

"Yes. It's just that I have no idea what my half of the tree will be, so if you have any ideas, let me know." She raised her voice so the girls could hear her too.

"Yes, Nana," Jade and Amber said in unison, and then they burst out in a fit of giggles. This pair was going to ruin the surprise if they weren't careful.

"How have you been doing?" Kathleen finally asked him. "Have they been good for you?"

"It's been a difficult week," he said. "Lois died two years ago yesterday. Though it was easier than last year. I guess it is true. Time heals."

"Or at least it adds distance and maybe some perspective," she said. "It's been three years since my divorce. The pain is getting less each year."

"Pat says I need to move on," he said, his voice cracking a little.

"I'm not sure if you need to move on so much as learn to live with the grief. It becomes part of you," she said. "Especially when you lose someone you grew up with."

"I hadn't thought of it that way," he said, pulling into the condo's underground parking. "Listen, I need to get some gas before it gets too busy down here. Can I drop you three off and then buzz when I'm back?"

She looked at him and at the fuel gauge, then peered at him with curiosity. *Damn.* The tank was nearly full.

"Sometimes the gauge is faulty," he said.

"You should get that fixed," she said, before opening the door and helping the girls down from the truck.

He drove away quickly toward the store and parked in the loading zone. Josh and the young woman who worked there,

Casey, rushed outside to help him unload.

They set the boxes on the counter, served the few customers still there over the dinner hour, and then looked into the boxes.

"Wow," Josh said. "These are great."

"Do you have everything you need, then?" asked Roy.

"Definitely. Kathleen's going to love this," said Casey. "We'll have it all ready when she comes by to lock up. I can't wait to see the look on her face."

Satisfied that his plan was in action, Roy drove back to the condo, parked, and rode the elevator to Kathleen's floor. When he got there, he was greeted by a pair of excited girls. They each took one hand and pulled him inside to see the view. "Look." Amber pointed out the window. "It's going to start soon."

"Not for another hour or so," said Kathleen from the kitchen. "First, let's have some lasagna, and then we can make some popcorn and hot cocoa and settle down to watch the show."

Roy walked into the galley kitchen to ask if he could help. She glared at him, and he backed off a bit. "What's wrong?" he asked.

"How dare you use the kids to get into my good graces again?" she whispered angrily. "You told me to get out, and now you've forced your way in here. What do you want, Roy?"

"I want to be friends again, Kathleen."

"Well, you have a pretty funny way of showing it," she said. "Using your grandchildren as pawns."

"I can see it looks that way, but really it isn't." He held his hands out to her, palms upward, hoping she would realize he was being sincere. "I wanted to say sorry about how I spoke to you the other day. I had the wrong end of the stick. Pat straightened me out."

"About what?"

"About Lois—how you had been angry with her for getting pregnant. And he told me that it was me, not him, you both cared about back then."

"It doesn't matter anymore, Roy. It's been decades. Let's just get through the next couple of weeks until Nic and Jason come home. Then we can go back to avoiding each other again."

"I don't want to avoid you," he said, stepping closer. "I want to get to know you again. We were friends for a long time, Kat. I think we can be friends again."

She opened her mouth to say something, but closed it again and shook her head.

"Could you at least try? I promise I won't talk about Lois all the time. Look." He held out his left hand. His ring finger was bare but for a clear tan line. "I took it off. I talked to her about it, and then I took it off."

"I'm glad you took it off. Maybe now you can find another woman to share your life with," she said softly. "I wish you every happiness."

"But don't you see? I haven't been happy. Something has been missing in my life for years. I filled the hole with Jason, with work, and even with Lois, but there's been something missing ever since you left."

"I had to leave," she said defensively.

"I know. I understand. But you're back now. I'm back. I just want us to be..."

"Friends again?" she asked, stepping toward the stove to remove the lasagna.

"Yes. To start with."

She placed the pasta on the stove and slowly turned toward him. "What do you mean, 'to start with'?"

He reached for her, pulled off the oven mitts she was wearing, and grasped each of her hands in his. "Kat, when you left after high school, you took a piece of me with you. I was angry. I was hurt that you never came back to visit. I didn't understand why. And then over the years I figured it was for the best. I had Lois and Jason and work, and that was enough for a long time. But still, in the back of my mind, I always wondered why you never visited and what Lois and I had done to make you leave."

"And now you know why I couldn't stay," she said.

"Yes. I never knew you cared about me like I cared for you. I didn't know why you and Lois fell out. I had no idea. I'm sorry."

She looked up at him and nodded slowly. "I forgive you," she said. "But I think we should eat before the show begins. I think the girls will enjoy it."

They ate their meal in silence, listening to the girls chatter. She looked up at him often, but when she noticed him watching her, she quickly looked down again. For his part, he was hopeful. Maybe, just maybe, they could put all the anger and hurt behind them and begin again.

They had just cleared the dishes and popped the popcorn when the sailboats began to parade past. "If you like, you can step out on the balcony and watch," Kathleen told the girls. "Just make sure you put your coats and gloves on. I'll bring out your hot chocolate as soon as it's done."

The girls scrambled into their warm clothes and stepped outside, clambering up onto the lounge chairs.

"It's a beautiful view from here," Roy said, looking at her. "I can see why you like it."

"And it's close to the store," she added. She was making small talk to avoid answering his earlier questions. He smiled and stepped closer, watching the girls out of the corner of his eye.

"Have you thought about what I said earlier? About being friends again?" He held his breath. He hadn't realized how much he wanted this until now.

"I'm not sure I can just be friends, Roy," she answered. "What if I want more? I don't want to be rejected again."

"We won't know unless we try," he said, stepping even closer to her. She smelled like home.

She shook her head. "Roy, we're at different places in our lives. I'm still working, and I don't want to quit yet. You're retired, and you must want someone who can be available full-time. I think it's best we just try to be civil like we promised the kids."

He took another step closer, and her face tilted up to him, and he waited for her to push back. To tell him to leave. To use her sharp tongue to cut him. Instead, she glanced out to the balcony where the girls were happily enjoying the parade and reached her hand around his neck, pulling his mouth toward hers.

This is going better than I'd hoped, he thought, before he placed his lips on hers and kissed her hard. She gave as good as she got, and he was sure he could stand like this for hours, tasting her and enjoying the scent of lavender in her hair.

She was the one to break the kiss and step back. "I've been wanting to see what that would be like," she said.

"And?" He smiled at her, hoping to put her at ease.

"Better than I remembered," she said, and he stepped toward her and pulled her into his embrace again.

"What are we going to do now?" he asked. "A moment ago, you thought we should stay civil. I'm confused."

"So am I—but I'm less confused when you're close by." She smiled. The kettle whistled, and she excused herself to make the hot cocoa and take it out to the girls. He watched her, and awaited her return.

She paused at the kitchen doorway to look at him and then stepped forward again. "I think we can give this a try, Roy. If you promise to stay civil. I don't want this to interfere with our family. I can't risk losing Nicole and the girls."

"That would never happen," he said. "I promise."

"Now come and see the fireworks," she urged. "Last year they were quite good."

CHAPTER 19

"What did you think of the sailpast?" Kathleen asked the girls, keeping her eyes on them and away from Roy. He was watching her every move, and his lips reminded her too much of the kisses they'd just shared. Kissing Roy Davies was the last thing she'd expected to do tonight, and now doing it again was all she could think about.

"It was great, Nana," said Amber.

"Is it time for the surprise yet, Grandpa?" Jade asked.

"What surprise?" asked Kathleen, turning toward Roy.

"The girls and I have been doing some work over the last couple of days. Tell you what—put on your warm coats, and we'll go take a look."

"The surprise is outside?" What were these three up to?

"Nope!" said Amber, but she covered her mouth when both Roy and Jade said, "Shhh!"

They all put on their coats, and Kathleen grabbed her purse to follow Roy out of the house.

"Best lock up," Roy said. "We may be a while."

What were they up to? After a short drive, they pulled up in front of the store. "We don't have to stop here tonight. I arranged for Josh to lock up."

"We aren't here to lock up," said Roy. They all climbed out, and the girls grabbed her hands and led her to the window. "Look, Nana!"

Kathleen looked at Roy, who had placed his hand on her shoulder and gestured toward the front window. Casey and Josh were looking out at her, smiling widely. "What are you up to?" she asked.

"The tree, Nana," said Amber. "Look at the tree."

Kathleen turned her attention toward the tree and gasped. "Oh my!"

The tree was covered in little white snowflakes, Santas, reindeer, and sleighs, all made from little plastic blocks. "Isn't this fabulous!" She scanned the scene before her again. "Oh, and look—you've made a toy store out of blocks. You're so clever." She turned to hug the girls and then Roy. "Thank you so much. You have no idea how much I have been worried about this theme."

"Oh, yes we do," said Jade. "You talk about it all the time."

Kathleen laughed. "I suppose I do. I'm so glad you thought of the answer. This is perfect!"

"Yep, building blocks and building gingerbread. All about building things!" said Jade.

"So it is," said Kathleen, happy that they had all been building things together the past few weeks, be it houses or bridges. It had brought them closer as a family. She hoped Nicole and Jason would be pleased.

CHAPTER 20

"They're here, they're here!" Jade and Amber skidded into the living room where Kathleen and Roy were enjoying a well-earned glass of wine beside the Christmas tree.

"Wonderful," said Kathleen. "You go out and meet them. They'll be happy to see you."

"And then we can open our Christmas Eve present?" asked Jade.

Kathleen laughed. "After your mom and dad are settled in and have time to put their feet up for a few minutes."

The two girls scampered off and were soon outside on the front porch gleefully exchanging greetings and hugs with their parents.

"We should probably go out and meet them," Kathleen said, not wanting to move. She was enjoying just being able to sit with him, no expectations, no need to come up with sparkling conversation.

It was comfortable and comforting.

"Yes, I suppose we should," he said, not moving from his spot, his arm on the sofa behind her.

The children and grandchildren were now in the house, and Jade's loud chatter could be heard from down the hall.

"Nana made sandwiches, and there's coffee and, oh, oh..."

"Sugar cookies," Amber finished for her.

"Amber, I wanted to tell them! We made sugar cookies and decorated them like snowmen, and we made gingerbread and..." Jade's voice was louder now as she scrambled to be the first to share everything.

"Did you make shortbread too?" That was Nicole's voice, just outside the door.

"Yes! And rum balls!" Jade said.

"Where is your grandfather?" Jason asked.

"And Nana?" Nicole asked. "We have a surprise for her." Kathleen could tell by her voice that Nicole was growing concerned about their absence.

"What kind of a surprise?" asked Jade.

"Can you keep a secret?" asked Jason.

"Yes!" Amber and Jade both screamed.

"Uncle Terrence is coming for Christmas. He'll be here tonight!"

"Yeah!"

"Shhh!" said Nicole. "It's a surprise, remember."

"Sounds like you have some acting to do later on," Roy said to Kathleen. "You'll have to look very surprised."

Kathleen raised her hand to wipe away a tear. "I'll be so glad to see him. He's been so angry with me. I just hope we can find some common ground."

"I'm sure he'll come around. He's managed to come to the island, which is a big step for him."

"We really should go in there and greet them now," she said to him, setting down her glass of mulled wine after taking another sip.

"If you insist." He stood and reached for her hand to pull her up. "But first there's something we need to do." He pulled her closer to the Christmas tree and bent to flick on the string of lights.

"That's a good idea," Kathleen said. "They'll like that."

"That wasn't exactly what I had in mind," Roy said, pulling her closer and pointing at the ceiling above him. "We need to break in the mistletoe."

She chuckled and leaned into his embrace. "You really do know how to say the right thing."

"They're in the living room," Amber said. "Nana told us to get you lunch, and then we can open presents. Come on!" Two pairs of small feet could be heard pelting down the hall to the kitchen.

"Do you think they got along while we were gone?" Nicole asked.

"I hope so," Jason answered from just outside the room.

In the periphery of her awareness, Kathleen heard a door opening, a gasp, and the door closing again.

"Well, I guess that answers that question. It looks like they're getting along just fine," Jason said, chuckling.

"Let's give them some time alone. I imagine they've earned it!" Nicole said from farther down the hall.

"We really should be joining them," Kathleen said when she broke the kiss.

Roy looked down at her, his eyes tender. "Yes, we probably should," he said. "But I think the mistletoe needs a little more use first, don't you?"

She nodded and wrapped her arms tighter around his neck, pulling his head down and kissing him again, happy to be just where she wanted and needed to be.

ABOUT THE AUTHOR

Jeanine Lauren has always loved a good story. She prefers those where the strength of community and the power of love combine to overcome even the darkest of situations.

Jeanine writes from her home in the lower mainland of British Columbia, Canada, not far from the fictional town of Sunshine Bay, where many of her characters live.

Christmas Trees and Mistletoe is Jeanine's fourth book.

Want to read more by Jeanine Lauren? Visit her website at jeaninelauren.com and join her newsletter to learn when her next books are available.

READ MORE OF JEANINE LAUREN'S BOOKS

Love's Fresh Start
Come Home To Love
Angel and the Neville Next Door

Printed in Great Britain
by Amazon

81286182R00174